Praise for Se

'This is a writer who k   it
place, poignant, someti￼   ;e
stories fit worlds into s￼   .'
Angela Readman – author of Don't Try This At Home

'Amanda's work is well crafted, subtle, and shows a deft hand. I love the way she gets into the psychology of each character, delving into their secret wishes and desires, giving us insights into how and why people act the way they do.'
A M Howcroft, InkTears – author of Nobody Will Ever Love You

'The writing is flawless and carefully shaded, the layers of meaning unfolding elegantly. Relationships and emotions are experienced at the peak of a single moment in the characters' lives.'
Joanna Campbell – author of When Planets Slip Their Tracks

'If you want the perfect witness to a crime, Amanda Huggins is your woman. She notices everything about the people, places and the things around her. Colours, temperature, sounds, the lot. And she gets all this down in lovely little stories that spin around in the readers' head, dizzying us with her powerful images of loss, regret and yearning.'
David Gaffney – author of All The Places I've Ever Lived

SEPARATED FROM THE SEA

Amanda Huggins

Retreat West Books
https://retreatwestbooks.com

Amanda Huggins lives in Yorkshire and works in engineering. *Separated From the Sea* is her first full-length short story collection. Her fiction and travel writing have been published in a number of literary journals, guidebooks and anthologies, as well as in magazines and newspapers including *The Guardian*, *Daily Telegraph*, *Mslexia*, and *Wanderlust*.

In 2014 Amanda won the British Guild of Travel Writers New Travel Writer Award, and her flash fiction collection, *Brightly Coloured Horses*, was published by Chapeltown Books in 2018.

Follow her on Twitter @troutiemcfish

CONTENTS

'T would be as wise to spend thy power
In trying to lure the bee from the flower,
The lark from the sky, or the worm from the grave,
As in weaning the Sea-Child from the wave.

Eliza Cook

SEPARATED FROM THE SEA

Long before the accident, Marnie's mam had asked Da to quit working on the trawlers and take a job in the smokehouse. Yet in her heart she'd always known he had no choice but to go to sea. The tug of the tide was a physical thing, woven into his being, and he could barely breathe if he stayed too long on the shore.

When she was asleep, Marnie understood this too; in her dreams Da inhabited the sea as though he were a fish. He swam away from his boat, down and deep through shoals of glittering herring, and he was smiling. But when she woke up she ran aground again without him. There was no one to sit at the foot of her bed and read her stories of the sea gods. When she tried to read them for herself, she discovered that the books were full of words she didn't understand. Sometimes, before the sadness of losing Da had all but silenced her, Mam had told Marnie folktales of her own. But her stories didn't shine. There were no mermaids or dolphins or sea sprites in them; they were inland stories of wolves and goblins, from the moors and woods near the town where she was brought up.

Marnie missed Da the most when she remembered their

9

special mornings together; those mornings when Mam had started work an hour early. When Marnie heard their alarm clock through the wall, she'd wrap herself in a blanket and curl up in the bedroom window, knees drawn up to her chin. She'd listen to the sounds of wheezing floorboards and clanky plumbing, and watch the sky for that precious hour when the brightest stars were still faintly visible in the dawn light.

After her mother had set off to work, Da would make them his special toast, spread with swirls of golden honey that he said were locks of mermaid hair. Before they left for school, he always crouched down to tie her boots, even though she'd been able to lace them herself since she was four years old. Then they'd head down to the shoreline to search for sea treasure; the flotsam of the night's tide laid out for the taking. Her father collected driftwood for the stove: twisted branches that had travelled across oceans, planks from shipwrecks with their paint peeling back in layers, and lengths of faded rope that he could re-use for his nets. But Marnie sought out the smooth pebbles, freckled like eggs, and the things the sea had taken from the land and sculpted into gems. Rounded fragments of broken pottery, dappled with faded patterns of flowers and birds, and shards of glass, rumbled into opaque nuggets of turquoise, emerald, cornelian and opal.

Da had another name for sea glass; he said Marnie was collecting sailors' souls. He told her that every bead of glass contained the soul of someone lost at sea: a fishermen or sailor or rigger, and that each piece took on the colour of the sailor's eyes. It was said a glass soul washing up on the strand was a sign that the spirit wished to return to shore as flesh and blood, but this could only come about if they were found by someone who had loved them.

But her mother didn't believe a word of Da's sea myths, and suggested that if Marnie believed them herself she would do well to take all the glass she had collected back down to the beach, so that others had a chance of reuniting with the lost souls of their departed.

Neither did her mam understand anything about sea life or birds. Da had taken Marnie for Sunday walks along the cliff tops, carrying her grandfather's old binoculars round his neck, and they had watched the terns and gulls that nested on the precarious ledges. Da once found a single unbroken egg, abandoned and half-hidden in bracken. Marnie carried it home wrapped in a handkerchief, and held it up against the light of her bedside lamp, trying to see through the thin shell and make out the half-formed bird; a bird that would never hear the wind or see the blue of the sky, and would never swoop and dive, or soar on the currents, or take in the glitter of the sea and the roll of a hill in a single moment.

And now, when she found a particularly beautiful shell, or saw a bird she couldn't identify, there was no one to show and no one to ask.

Marnie found herself contained by new boundaries; those of her mother's world. Her mam spent the evenings listening to the radio, and while she listened she embroidered, decorating dress collars and handkerchiefs with daisies and roses and forget-me-nots. Marnie asked if she would stitch her bedroom curtains with cockleshells, sea thrift, and mermen, but her mother could not invent or ad-lib, she could only follow the printed outlines on the cloth, or trace a pattern from a magazine, and these didn't include mythical creatures or things that came from the sea.

Her mam wasn't like the other women in the village. She

came from inland, from a town overshadowed by the moors, and she knew little of fishing. Her family had lived in a narrow house in the old town, with tall windows that flaunted glimpses of heathered hills through gaps between the terraces. She had won a scholarship to the grammar school, and all the girls there had parents who worked in offices and banks, and lived in semi-detached houses on the outskirts of town. Marnie's mother decided she wanted that too.

'But then she met me and all else was forgotten,' Da used to tease. 'She turned my head when I saw her at the fairground that day, and I wasn't going to let her slip through my fingers.'

And when she moved to the village she took a job at the bank, and kept herself apart from the other women. The fishermen's wives and widows helped out with the nets and worked in the herring sheds. Met in the village hall on Thursdays to knit sweaters for their men and gossip over tea and cake. When they saw Mam walking past in her suit and high heels, they might nod in acknowledgement, but they'd never speak to her.

When the accident happened there were four other fishermen who died alongside her da. Their widows came round to the cottage and asked Mam if she needed anything, but she just shook her head and went back inside. And everywhere she went, Marnie could hear the village whispering; a faint murmur like the distant sea at low tide. You could hear it in the newsagent and the local Co-op, and no one ever came to the house any more, except for Louise.

Louise was Mam's friend, and she'd known her since school. For as long as Marnie could remember she had come down from the town to visit. The two of them used to go out to The Anchor, for what Louise called a 'proper girls' chat', but now that Da wasn't there to watch Marnie, they stayed in and drank wine from tumblers at the kitchen table. They talked quietly while Marnie watched TV in the parlour. Sometimes she crept to the door and watched them through the hole in the latch. After a few drinks her mother always started to cry and then Louise would say that they should move back to the town, into the empty house that had belonged to Mam's parents.

They had visited that house sometimes when her nana was still alive. The walls were panelled with laminate, patterned like wood but cold to the touch, and there was a gas fire in the parlour that reckoned to look just like real coals. Nana said it was a blessing, but Marnie could see that it was a fire without a soul. The house was cold and mean, and too far from the sea. A handful of gulls flew those few miles inland and wheeled above the town in search of scraps. Their cries seemed louder away from the crash of the sea; plaintive voices trapped in the dank valley between the moors.

Marnie was scared that her mother would listen to Louise, and they would have to move to the town, yet she couldn't find the words to tell her how much she wanted to stay close to the sea. Mam would never understand that when she heard the waves, she could hear Da's voice.

Every morning, Mam watched her leave for school through the parlour window. Marnie waved when she reached the corner, then dodged back through the ginnels and walked along the shoreline as she'd always done. She still scoured the sand for treasure, yet now she only picked out the nuggets of brown and ochre glass, occasionally tricked by the shine of a scrap of seaweed. Da's eyes had been the colour of amber, flecked with marmalade and sunshine. There was no glass to match them, yet still she held each piece in her palm, closing her eyes until she could feel his calloused hand in hers. But the glass always remained cold. Marnie threw them all back into the sea, hurling the glass as far and as hard as she could, as though to discourage each piece from washing ashore again, only for her to repeat the same disappointment. She knew that Da couldn't be found on the shore. She'd have to swim out to sea if she wanted to find him.

The following Monday morning, for the first time since the accident, her mother set off for work early, leaving Marnie's breakfast laid out for her on the table. Underneath the newspaper she found a letter from a removal firm with a quotation for moving their things to the narrow house in the town. She put it back where she'd found it and carried her pots over to the sink. From the kitchen window she could see the soft grey swell of the sea. Today would be the day she'd find Da.

She went back upstairs and pulled on her favourite swimming costume underneath her jeans and jumper, then left the cottage and crossed the road to the coble landing. She took nothing with her, not even a towel. She walked down the slipway to the sand, along the shoreline towards the lighthouse and the pier. There was no one around. The day was drab and dull, and scudding clouds threatened squally rain. Beyond the pier, she saw her father's friend, George, starting up the old tractor to drag his dinghy up the beach. She waved, but he didn't see her.

She slipped off her clothes, and left them folded neatly on the sand with her house key tucked inside her red jumper. Then she waded out to Jackson's Rock, to where the seabed fell away sharply, and the water darkened. At first the cold stole her breath from her, but the deeper she went the less she could feel it. A man shouted to her from the pier, and the rushing tide sucked and hissed and churned the sand, threatening to topple her before she reached the rock. Yet when the moment came, Marnie smiled as she disappeared beneath the spume and spindrift, because now she would never be separated from the sea. The tide was ready to take her to Da, and she had no choice but to go.

THE VIEW THROUGH RAIN

It's only eight-thirty, and I know I won't sleep until you return. Rain is drumming on the metal ducting outside the window, amplifying my jet lag. I hear heavy footsteps and, for a moment, I think it's you. Then an apartment door opens across the corridor, and there's the murmur of a television before it shuts again.

I decide to go out even though I haven't brought a coat. I remember New York being warmer than this at the end of May. I think about the last time we were here together, when I tied up my hair with the blue silk scarf you bought for me in Bloomingdales.

Across Eighth Avenue, the neon sign blinks on and off above Tony's Bar & Grill; a plaid shirt and work boots kind of bar, strangely out of place in midtown Manhattan. I buy a two-dollar hot dog from the cart outside your building and eat it in the shelter of the doorway. Then I dash across the road as the light changes to green, splashing through wet puddles, cold against my bare legs. I push open the door to Tony's and drop my umbrella in the stand.

Music plays, turned down low; the singer has lost his

woman, his job and his home.

I knew you'd leave, and let the screen door slam on our love, you never did believe . . .

A group of men are sat talking at the bar, drinking beer and lining up bourbon chasers. I can hear the click of pool balls in the back room. I take my beer, leave a dollar tip, and sit at a long table by the window. I watch the passers-by, their collars turned up against the rain, stepping on the neon letters flashing pink on the wet pavement. I kick off my damp shoes and stretch my toes.

As I look across the street I see you. You have a folded newspaper held over your head. Your suit jacket is soaked, hanging limp, and I can already imagine the smell of damp wool as it hangs to dry over a chair back.

You dash under the door canopy, and pause for a minute, looking down at your wet brogues. You appear smaller than I remember. Narrower. Your face is pale, pinched, and your hair sticks damply to your forehead. Maybe New York is too big for you. I see you as a stranger would: impartial, unmoved. My heart does not beat harder, faster. You are just another middle-aged man, hunched in the rain. I reach for my phone, to call and tell you to come across to the bar. But something stops me. I don't want to see you yet.

A man walks over to my table as I put the phone back into my pocket. He holds two shots of whisky, and places one in front of me. I look up, and he smiles.

'Carl,' he says, holding out his hand. 'You need something warm on a night like this. And this ain't no place for a lady to sit all alone. I thought you may need company?'

I feel sure that this must be some kind of bet. But when I glance over at the bar, his friends all have their backs to us, elbows still resting on the counter. I look across the street, but you've already gone inside.

'I'm waiting for someone,' I say to him.

He smiles again and sits down opposite me. 'Now correct me if I'm wrong, but I was watching you just now as you looked out of that window, and I'm guessing that things look kinda different from this side of the street.'

I know I should make my excuses and leave, but somehow this is where I want to be right now, here in this run-down bar, at a table branded with stale beer rings, talking to a stranger in scuffed cowboy boots.

His skin is tanned and weathered, shoulders broad, and his shirt sleeves are pushed up muscled forearms. He tells me he's from Kansas, here for the next six months working on a construction site in Hell's Kitchen. He tells me he likes my accent, and says he means to visit London one day.

He fetches two more whiskies and two more beers. While he's at the bar I check my phone, but there are no missed calls or messages from you.

When he comes back I tell him about you, your work assignment over here, that we've been apart for two months. How you weren't there to meet me at the airport because you had to stay at the office for a meeting. How the doorman had to let me into the apartment.

I don't tell him how lonely I felt while I waited there for you, or about the letter from Jennifer that I found last week when I was looking for my passport. You'd promised me that it was over, but now I can't be sure any more.

I don't tell him how I felt when I saw you earlier across the street, or how I suddenly knew that something had been irrevocably lost. A subtle shift that only became clear when it was refracted through the rain.

Carl tells me about his wife, Ellie, and about their still-born baby boy. How she sat on the porch step every night, staring into the darkness. How they stopped talking, and how she looked straight through him as though he were nothing more than a shadow. This is why he decided to come to New York for a few months. He sends Ellie money each week, and writes a letter, but she never replies.

He doesn't need to tell me how sad this makes him.

When I look outside again, the rain has stopped, and the puddles are a jumble of bright reflections.

Carl asks if I'd like to go for a walk. He takes my hand, and we cross the avenue to Forty-Eighth Street. Crowds are drifting out of the theatres and wandering along the shining, wet pavements, laughing and chatting.

When we reach Times Square, we stop. And amidst the towers of neon and the snake of yellow cabs, we hear jazz music drifting from a tiny doorway between two shops. We stand and listen for a while, hand in hand: the cowboy and the English girl. Wishing. Then we walk slowly back again, and he leaves me at the corner. There is nothing else to say that won't lead to somewhere we can't go. We part with a single kiss.

I stand there for a moment on the corner of the block, wishing that I could follow him back to the bar. I step towards the kerb, but your doorman sees me and calls out. I know what I must do, so I turn round and come back into your building, my step suddenly heavy.

You don't look up straight away when I walk into the apartment. You finish typing something on your laptop and quickly close it. Then, finally, you smile and stand up and hold out your arms to me. I think of how I felt when I watched you through the rain, and I know that Carl is sitting in Tony's right now, looking out across the same street.

BROKEN CROW

At the far end of the field, where the wooden fence ends and the barbed wire starts, Evie sees something flutter. Something's caught up in the wire. It's too far away for her to make out clearly, but she's certain that it's alive. A bird, she decides, a large one, black as soot. A crow? It flaps a wing, then drops it in defeat, then flaps again. The other wing is caught fast, appearing to hang in a tatter of broken feathers.

She watches for a minute, then moves slowly around the cottage, her feet mired in reluctance as she fetches her jacket and gloves, her penknife, and the kitchen scissors. They might be useless tools against the thick wire, but they are all she has, and she is compelled to try and free the crow.

What will she do if the bird is beyond help? Her heart quickens, fear flapping inside her rib cage like the crow's tangled wing. She won't be able to kill it, she knows that. She'll have to call someone.

A row of blackthorn bushes run between the path and the far edge of the field, and she can't see the wire fence from her approach. As she gets closer, she remembers the two sparrows that danced in front of her car that time. Parents perhaps, with chicks in the nest, waiting for food. They swooped across the lane in front of her, then the female made a sudden turn, and thudded against the windscreen. Evie cried out, but she didn't stop - couldn't stop - to see if the bird was alive. She still pictures it now, lying in the road, suffering, dying, and the male bird fluttering wildly above.

The freeing of this broken crow will be her reparation for the bird she killed.

As she emerges from the end of the hedge, she can see it clearly for the first time: her crow is a tattered black bin bag wrapped around the wire, shredded into torn feathers.

She leans against the stile for a moment, relieved, and yet a part of her still wishes there was a bird to save. Without the crow there can be no absolution, and the sparrow will continue to fly into the blackness of the windscreen, again and again.

NOISE

Is it true that only a suicide stops a Japanese train from running on time?

Sophia frowned, tucking her father's postcard back into her bag. Why did he always ask questions like this?

She finished her coffee and looked around. The cafe was usually busy, yet today it was almost empty. For the first time she was aware of the sun pouring in through the windows and realised the season had changed without her noticing. Most people were outside, feeling the warmth of the summer sun on their skin. She stood up to leave, and the staff called out their thanks in unison: four ringing voices rising above the hiss of the coffee machine and the background jazz.

'Arigato gozaimasu!'

Sophia found it hard to tune out the everyday clamour of Japanese life: the cuckoo signals at pedestrian crossings, the genial J-pop and chirpy adverts blaring out from every shop, and the cacophonous din of the pachinko parlours. Even in the countryside there was noise. Muzak and jingles were piped through tannoys in the village streets, drifting out to the rice paddies, warding off the terror of silence. When Sophia travelled to Onokatsu to visit the temples, she asked the elderly woman in the noodle shop why they didn't complain. The woman shrugged and said that there was nothing to be done. It was not to be questioned, it was just part of life.

And at night in the city, the lights added an extra layer of silent noise; a busy, bright chatter of flashing neon inside Sophia's head.

***

When Paul first announced he'd been offered a transfer from London to Tokyo, part of her had held back, wanting to say no. Yet she knew he thought it was time to go, and that the move would be good for them both.

He could no longer face seeing Sophia's grief, yet she understood that Paul had simply stored away his own, and he'd buried it so deep that there were no longer any surface ripples. She knew the loss of a child wasn't something to 'get over'; it wasn't a hurdle to leap and leave behind. It was a defining line; a line from which everything would be measured from now on: the time before Calum's death, and the time after Calum's death. Grief had already become a part of the warp and weft of her, yet at random moments it would rear up unexpectedly with a clatter of hooves, and when it did, the noise was deafening. And unlike the everyday clamour of Tokyo, the noise of grief couldn't be silenced by earplugs or soundproofing.

***

They'd flown to Tokyo three weeks before Paul started work, and on their second weekend they took a trip to a hot spring resort. After dinner in their room they made love on the tatami floor, a red silk kimono spread out beneath them. It wasn't urgent or hurried, like the brief couplings they had sought to try and block out death; those violent, bruising encounters that felt like bone on bone. It was slow and considered, and it confirmed, without words, that things could be good again.

On their final evening there was a firework festival in the village. They walked through fields in the fading light, following the lanterns that bobbed ahead of them in a dancing line of turquoise, green and amber. They spread rugs out on the grass, and when the rockets filled the sky with bursts of gold and red, the children breathed a soft collective sigh, and the adults smiled and held their hands. No one noticed Sophia's tears, and even she herself wasn't quite sure whether they were being shed for her loss or her happiness.

But this fledgling happiness was short-lived. Paul worked long hours, and rarely took holidays. Sophia was expected to attend dinners with his British and American colleagues, but she found them unbearable. The men were self-important and rude to waiters. Their wives were brittle creatures with helmet hair and clunky jewellery. They spent their days shopping and lunching, and in the evenings they moved their expensive food around on bland restaurant plates and clawed at their husbands' arms with their scarlet nails. Sophia thought up reasons not to go, until Paul eventually stopped passing on her excuses, and finally she was forgotten.

After a while she no longer felt out of place in Tokyo on her own. She explored the streets and parks and galleries, the temples and the teahouses, and drank coffee in her favourite cafe in Shibuya. As the world strode by the cafe window, Sophia looked on with calm detachment, and when she was tired of looking she wrote everything down in her journal.

She wrote about their neighbour, Mrs Takahashi, who would knock on Sophia's door and leave a jar of homemade bean jam or a bag of anpan buns outside on the step. She recounted her walks through the city, and wrote about the man she glimpsed changing his shirt in the doorway at the back of a shop. He revealed a torso that was a riot of fish, flowers, geisha and warriors: the ink badges of a yakuza gangster. He was as colourful as the street fashionistas, but just like the Harajuku girls, his attempt at diversity only reinforced his conformity. And she described the row of shoes - a man's, a woman's, and a small girl's - that she saw lined up inside an open doorway. Sophia imagined the family, laughing and talking over dinner, and the daughter, sleepy-eyed, as her mother kissed her goodnight. More than ever, she felt a dull ache for the different life that she'd lost.

And she wrote of her longing for silence, and of how only suicide prevented a Japanese train from running on time.

She didn't write about Paul; how he drank every night after work in the hostess bars, and entertained clients in the geisha district. She didn't mention that she sat on her own in their apartment, waiting for him to come home while she listened to the neighbour's TV through the thin walls. She didn't talk about how sad this made her. And Sophia never wrote about Akiro.

She met him one evening when she was walking through the backstreets in Shinjuku. He was taking a cigarette break, standing in the doorway of his bar, when he saw her peering up the staircase through the tangle of overhead cables. She was wondering which of the tiny bars to venture into, reading the neon signs that flashed above the doors. He bowed, and ushered her upstairs with a sweep of his arm. She ducked her head under a low beam as she went in through the metal door and sat down on the nearest bar stool. She was the only customer. Akiro told her his name, and asked Sophia hers, as he put down a clean beer mat and a hot towel. Then he poured her a beer, and lined up two small dishes of rice crackers. She drank the beer too fast and watched the black and white Kurosawa film that was playing silently on a screen behind Akiro's head. He looked up at her and smiled, and opened two more bottles of beer. And around ten o'clock, when no one else had come in, he quietly locked the door.

She went back to see him the following week, but there was a Japanese woman with him behind the bar, and he pretended not to know her.

Sophia understood that all the city could offer her was a different sadness, akin to a constant feeling of jet-lag, that left her disoriented and light-headed. She was blinded by Tokyo's density. There were no panoramic views; only a set of close-ups at point blank range.

***

And so Sophia began to measure out her life in Japan with a daily routine of coffee shops and art galleries, trying to quieten the din and clatter inside her head with the hush of museums and books. Yet today, in the cafe, she realised she'd stopped noticing the seasons, the changes in the light; she had stopped observing real life.

And late on that hot July afternoon, Sophia took her usual route from the cafe in Shibuya to the train station. But she'd already decided not to go home. Instead, she would take a train to Sumida, to the Skytree tower. She'd eat her dinner there, high above Tokyo, and watch the city lights blink like gimcrack stars as the day faded. It was that time of year when the heavy-limbed heat of the afternoon rolled seamlessly into the evening, and it felt to Sophia as though something intoxicating was waiting just out of reach behind every sliding door. She knew that if she slid back those screens the reality would be a million ordinary Tokyo lives: a million men and women pouring each other a cold beer, cranking up the air-con, and talking about the good things and the bad things at the fag end of their day.

Yet she was sure that high above the city she would find silence.

She walked to the end of the station platform where it was less crowded, turning abruptly as she heard a commotion behind her. Somehow a baby buggy had fallen between the tracks. Sophia hardly hesitated; she jumped straight down, diving for the baby like a twenty-first century kamikaze pilot.

And although she wasn't in a position to notice, she would have been happy to learn that after the train screeched to a halt there was a moment of strange calm and stillness; a silence before the shouts and sirens. And her father would have been interested to hear she'd delayed the 16.56 by thirty-three minutes, and that all the trains on that line had run late for the next hour.

***

Sophia became an instant celebrity. The baby's parents asked to meet her, and when she declined they sent gifts instead. But Sophia didn't want thanks or presents, she already had the thing she needed. When she'd handed the child up to the waiting crowd, his dark eyes had met hers, weighing her up in that split second before deciding whether to laugh or cry. In that moment she had seen her own boy, and it was as though she had somehow balanced the scales: a child lost and a child saved.

And one morning, without telling Paul or leaving a note, she packed a bag and took the train to Onokatsu. She walked up the hill to the temple lodgings, and they agreed that she could take a room for as long as she needed.

On the second evening, Kimiko, the cook, asked Sophia to walk down to the pond with her to watch the fireflies. She told her of the Japanese belief that the tiny lights were the souls of soldiers who had died in battle. She brought her sister's two children with her, a boy and a girl, and they caught the glowing beetles in glass jars. They held them up for a few moments, captivated, before releasing them again, and as each insect found freedom the children called goodbye in their sweet singsong voices.

Sophia felt as though the lights were the departing soul of her own child, and as she watched them disappear she knew that something within her had shifted.

She slept well that night, yet she was awake again at dawn, because as she'd already discovered, the temple was as full of sound as the city. Outside her room she could hear the dry scrabble of birds' feet in the guttering, the papery whir and flutter of their tiny brown wings, and the cheeps of fledglings in the nest. When she walked in the fields, she was enveloped in the buzz and rasp and thrum of insects, and the rustle of dry grass. At dusk there were the temple bells, the soft lull of the monks' chants, and the gentle clink of pots and pans from the kitchen below her window.

And in this new noise, Sophia found her silence.

GIDDY WITH IT

On Saturday mornings we coveted satin flares and smock tops in Chelsea Girl; twirling feather boas until neon-bright plumes spiralled to the floor, testing plum-pout lipsticks on puckered lips. We'd claim a window seat at the Wimpy Bar and order milky coffees served in smoked glass beakers, then bitch about the girl with the Linda McCartney hair, and wave at the glam-rock boys in their platform boots from Daisy Roots.

But in the afternoons we were the band. We became Voodoo Velvet, chewing biro ends as we wrote our songs, scattering loose-leaf lyrics across your bed. We doodled stars in the margins, hearts and arrows, flowers strewing petals – he loves me, he loves me not.

We made drums from dented Quality Street tins, and fashioned drumsticks from pencils tipped with plasticine. I play-play-played those battered drums until I was giddy, and you strummed an old guitar rescued from the skip; that wreck-necked guitar with only five strings.

You taped it all on your dad's reel-to-reel: my unsure voice, the dum-dum-thrum of the plasticine, our hesitant laughter and the slip-slide-scratch of the steel strings. We borrowed your brother's records and played obscure B-sides turned down low, writing new words to the old tunes, and singing our cosmic lyrics over sixties beats. And then we'd dance to the radio, long-limbed and snake-hipped, until we were as dizzy as spun candy floss.

We'd stretch out on the rug with bottles of Coke and your mum's ham sandwiches, your Bolan hair a crazy tangle and my pale-sky jeans embroidered with palm trees and flowers.

Then one Sunday morning your brother found the Lou Reed LP we'd scratched, and he took the guitar and smashed it in half. I could hear tears in your voice when you told me, and I bit my lip until I drew blood. But your tears weren't for the guitar. He'd taken the reels too, twisting and stretching the tapes until they were all destroyed. You were breathless with the pain of it; I could hear it in your throat.

We still wrote our songs after that, but we never sang or played again, and our doodled hearts were wrapped in barbed wire. The Linda McCartney girl started coming into town with us, but you didn't tell her about the band, and we stopped going back to your house. We spent Saturday afternoons wandering along the seafront and following the Bowie-boys around the arcades. When my dad got transferred to York we wrote for a while, but I never saw you again.

Years later I'd tell people I used to be in a rock group; that we wore velvet flares and glitter on our cheekbones.

'Songs? Yeah, of course we wrote our own songs. Band members? Just the two of us; me and Chrissie. We were giddy with it all. We could have gone places, you know?'

ENOUGH

Evie found a cottage to rent beyond the northern edge of town, in the close-mouthed hinterland where the street-lights ran out. She liked the outskirts of a place; in sight of town, yet near to the foxes and the rustle of the unseen. It was shouting distance from the sea, but she couldn't hear the waves. The tides were silent and swift. She'd forgotten the silence, the water so far out, the endless grey reaches of shifting sands and mud flats. People admired the view: the vastness of the bay and sky, the distant Cumbrian crags crouched beneath threatening cloud, those wide sunsets. But to Evie the view had always seemed insubstantial and elusive, a wash of drab and dun. If you tried to capture it on camera, it receded further, as though it had never been anything more tangible than a dull mirage.

This was the town where she grew up, but everyone was a stranger now, which was just as she'd hoped. Everything else was as she'd left it; the same cafes and discount shops and bingo halls, their windows coated with the briny skin of the sea. The Midland Hotel had been refurbished a few years back, but Evie could see that it was already curling at the edges again. Eventually the salt air claimed everything back.

She told herself she would be happy here this time. The cottage she'd found was down a narrow lane off the coastal road, hunched between sycamore trees in the grounds of a large Victorian house that had been converted into a nursing home. And it came with its own transport - a hulk of a push-bike that had been left in the outhouse by an artist who had lived there before her.

Although the cottage was small, she felt there was space to breathe, and it would be enough. Two rooms, sparsely furnished: one up, one down, heated by a wood burner, and a fan heater that rattled like a bag of nails. It was the beginning of summer when she moved in, so she planned to collect enough wood before winter to see her through to spring.

When she cycled to work, she rarely rode along the promenade, but wound through the back streets instead, picking up broken chairs from skips, and fruit boxes scrounged from the greengrocer. She carried scissors and string in her rucksack, and Trevor laughed when she arrived at the cafe each day with her latest finds.

There was an axe and a rusty saw in the understairs cupboard, and she chopped the wood into uniform sizes and stacked it at either side of the stove. When the fireplace was full, she stored the rest in the outhouse, for which she bought a large padlock.

At weekends, if she had money for petrol, she'd drive her old car out into the countryside and scavenge for more wood. And, sometimes, if she asked the local farmers they would give her any broken pallets that were lying around.

She found two large ceramic pots in the yard, and planted seeds that she took from the nursing home greenhouse. The shoots grew tall and feathery-leaved, their tight buds opening into deep pink flowers with yellow hearts that made her smile. They waved on delicate stems, and she snipped off the dead flowers and watched tiny new buds grow in their place.

Work in the cafe seemed to suit her. Trevor paid her cash for making milkshakes and sandwiches, for wrestling with the Gaggia, and for constructing banana splits. And when the leaves started to fall, the windows were already steamed up by ten in the morning. The regulars took to their padded jackets and tweed caps, and occasionally she saw one of them slip out a hip flask of whisky and pour a measure into his tea.

She asked Trevor about the fire - about paper twists and firelighters, long matches, and ways of stacking logs and kindling. She started to use the fan heater in the evenings, but vowed not to light the fire until November.

He sent her home with leftover cakes and bread, and slices of ham and smoked salmon that had darkened at the edges. She rarely cooked, as she only had a two-ring hotplate and a toaster. There was a chip shop at the far end of the promenade, and sometimes she'd buy a battered fish as a treat and carry it home tucked inside her jacket.

Evie saved any spare money in her mother's tin. When she was a child, the tin held the antiseptic, the blue iodine bag for wasp stings, the neatly rolled bandages, and an array of plasters. It was the tin that stung and mended, the tin that made everything a little worse before it got better. And now it was her money tin, and she tucked it behind the pile of logs at the side of the stove.

On her days off she walked along the promenade, and watched families eating their lunch in the restaurant at the Midland, gazing out through the curved windows at the wide blue and the flat grey. Their mouths moved methodically as they ate, but there seemed to be little conversation. Their eyes were fixed on the distant nothing. She was sure they privately yearned to be outside, where they could hear the cry of the gulls and feel the whip of the salt air.

Evie borrowed books from the library, and read them in the launderette, and occasionally when she arrived back home around dusk, she would see a white-haired woman standing in a top floor window of the nursing home, waving and smiling. But if she waved back, the woman dropped her hand and turned away.

It was a straightforward life, and Evie loved that it was a life where it was possible to keep a distance. She was careful not to make friends or to raise anyone's curiosity, even though it no longer mattered. She had stopped worrying about whether Tony would try to find her. She knew he wouldn't. He hadn't loved her as much as she'd hoped, and neither had any of the others before him.

Somehow it was never enough.

When it got colder at the start of November, she lit the fire every evening, and sometimes she took Trevor's leftover sandwiches to two homeless men who slept in the stone bus shelter at the road junction. She started making up a flask of soup for them as well, and they would sit and talk to her while they drank it.

In December, the snow came, turning quickly to ice on the pavements and the side roads, and Evie took her duvet downstairs and slept on the couch by the fire.

Three days before Christmas, the two homeless men were given rooms in one of the hostels, but when Evie came home from work she saw there was already someone else in their place. She walked back down to the corner with a flask of soup, just as the snow started to fall again. She grasped the frosty railing at the edge of the path, the wool of her glove sticking to the metal. For a moment she thought the man had gone, and part of her was relieved, but then she saw he was still there, huddled in the corner of the shelter.

As Evie crossed the road she lost her footing, the flask crashed to the ground with her, and when she unscrewed the lid, the soup was a mess of glass. She considered turning round without saying anything. After all, it made no difference now.

But the man called out to her, asked if she was ok.

'I made you soup,' she said.

He nodded, as though he had been expecting her.

'Don't I know you?' he asked.

She shrugged and sat down, pulling her scarf up over her face, just in case he did recognise her from somewhere. He had layers of cardboard stuffed inside his coat, and a green hat pulled low over his ears.

He held up a bottle of whisky, and laughed. 'Never mind about the soup. This'll keep me warmer.'

Evie peered at him, trying to map a human face through stubble and dirt. His eyes were dark. She'd seen those eyes before, somewhere in another time.

'Here,' he said, offering the bottle, 'pour some into your flask cup.'

He talked quietly, his voice raspy. There was something in the lilt that was almost familiar to her, perhaps altered beyond recognition by the roll-ups and the whisky.

As he lifted the bottle to his lips again, she noticed the tattoo on his hand. A faded rose at the base of his thumb. Her heart lurched, but she said nothing. Jack. Jack Noble.

She saw his tanned skin, his arm flung above his head, his dark eyelashes resting on his cheek as he slept at her side in the warm meadow grass. She was only seventeen; he was only eighteen. She could smell the hot motorcycle engine, and see the shimmering road stretching ahead through that long summer. Her cowboy.

She handed him the flask cup. 'Keep it,' she said. 'I've got to go.'

As Evie left, she didn't turn round, but they both knew she would be back. They were both adrift in the hinterland.

***

Trevor was used to Evie lingering over a coffee after she'd finished her shift, savouring the cafe's warmth before she went home, waiting for the leftover food at closing time. But the next day she disappeared as soon as the clock chimed five, calling in at the camping shop for a new flask on the way home.

She lit the fire first, then made soup and wrapped up sandwiches and cake. Today she would find out why Jack Noble was homeless, and what he'd done with his life. She had so many questions.

When she got to the shelter, Jack was hunched on the bench, and his eyes were red and watery. Evie touched his forehead and it was hot and damp.

'You're coming to the cottage - no argument.'

She dragged him up and took his rucksack, and they walked slowly along the lane to the back gate.

'Are you sure about this? A strange man in your house?' He tried to laugh, but the sound splintered and turned into a cough.

'You aren't a stranger.'

'You remembered,' he said, but he didn't smile.

Evie put more logs on the fire, and Jack perched on the edge of the couch, holding out his chapped hands towards the flames. She poured the soup and found some paracetamol.

'Here, take these to bring your temperature down.'

She chatted as she cooked their supper, but Jack remained quiet, searching in his rucksack for tobacco and papers, scarcely answering her questions. He was just down on his luck, he said. He'd split up with his girlfriend and moved out of their flat, but had a mate finding him a place to live in a week or two, and the promise of a job.

She put his plate on a tray so he didn't have to leave the fire, and handed him a glass of wine. He drank it in gulps, and ate his omelette quickly, and in-between mouthfuls he got up and fed the stove with logs, as though he had some primal need to keep the flames roaring.

After they had finished the wine, they drank the remainder of Jack's whisky. They sat in silence, watching the fire, and Evie knew better than to ask him any more questions.

'If you like, you can stay here until your friend has a flat sorted out,' she said eventually. 'It's Christmas in two days' time - you can't spend Christmas Day on the streets.'

'I can't promise anything,' he said, as though it were he, not Evie, who was thinking of offering up a place to stay. 'Do you mind if I take a shower?'

When he went upstairs, she stretched his jacket out to dry over the back of a chair, and moved it closer to the fire. She heard the water run for a few minutes and then his footsteps moving around the tiny bathroom. Then there was silence.

When Jack didn't come down, Evie went up to the top of the stairs, and saw that the bedroom doorway was open. His shape was clearly visible under the duvet. She walked across the room and turned on the lamp. He didn't stir, and she sat down on the bed, watching him sleep, just as she had before.

His face was thinner now, hard-edged and gaunt beneath weathered skin, his hair curling damply across his forehead. When he didn't move, she slipped off her jumper and jeans and climbed in at his side, not touching him, just feeling the heat from him, and remembering the force of their passion.

***

Evie had a boyfriend when she first met Jack. Kind, predictable Aidan: the boy next door. But it wasn't enough. Jack glittered with danger, and when he gave her a lift home one evening, she invited danger inside.

After that first time, he often came round to see her in the early hours of the morning, when he was sure she was alone. In the half-dark, their tangled limbs blended into one; a single shade of pale. One night, she held her arm against his to show him.

'In the dark all cats are grey,' he said.

She laughed, and said she was happy they were one cat; that she was a part of him, and he of her.

'Our differences are only removed for a while, Evie. In the morning light they will become clear again.'

She shook her head. 'We have no differences, Jack - we're the same, you and I.'

He didn't answer, but stood up in one lithe movement and leant his elbows on the window sill as he looked out across the rooftops. She lay back on the pillow and heard the heavy clunk of his lighter as he flicked it open, and the deep intake of breath as he lit a cigarette. She wanted it to be enough, yet she wasn't sure.

And when he asked her to choose, she was scared, and so she chose Aidan, because she thought he loved her more. But it was too late to choose, because Aidan had found out about Jack, and it turned out that neither of them thought she was worth fighting for.

***

Evie reached over to switch off the lamp. As soon as the room was in darkness, Jack pulled her to him.

'You were awake?' she said.

'Of course. I was waiting for you, Evie.'

She forgot the promise she had made to herself to keep a distance. For the first time, she knew for certain that she could make this life be enough.

***

When she woke, it was barely light, her head was banging from the wine and whisky, and the bed was empty.

There was no sign of Jack downstairs, and his coat wasn't on the chair. She could see straight away that there were other things missing: the TV, the stereo, and her handbag. She opened the cupboards. Nearly everything was missing that he could use or sell. Even her library books had gone. She reached to the back of the fireplace for her mother's tin, but she knew before she did so that it wouldn't be there.

She opened the door to the yard. The outhouse door was swinging in the wind. She peered inside. Her bike was still there, but the logs had been taken. Then she realised that the car had gone too. Of course, how else could he have carried everything?

Evie fell to her knees in the snow and howled at the crows in the sycamore trees. They took flight, cawing and screeching as they flapped their untidy wings, and when she turned to watch them disappear over the big house, she saw the white-haired woman in the top floor window, pointing and laughing.

SEA GLASS

Alfie held out two pieces of pale blue sea glass, rumbled smooth by a thousand tides.

'These are the souls of fishermen lost at sea.'

'My da was lost at sea,' Cathy said. 'I don't remember him at all.'

Alfie looked doubtful, but she had already crouched down on the sand again, so she didn't notice.

'What 'bout these smaller pieces of glass?' she asked, scooping up a handful of wet sand that was speckled with chips of emerald and amber.

'They're the eyes of ships' cats,' he said. 'Cats who ventured up on deck and were swept overboard by freak waves, or who lost their footing on the rigging. If you match a pair of eyes, and sleep with them under your pillow, then the cat'll find his way back to land.'

'You're a liar, Alfie Machin!'

'No, you're the liar, Cathy Mainprize. Everyone knows it were Marnie's da who was lost at sea. Your da lives at 17 Castlegate with Vera Cappleman, and works on a trawler out of Whitby.'

Cathy's eyes grew round, but she continued to fill her pockets with sea glass.

When she got home, she told her mam what Alfie had

41

said about Da. Mam paused at the sink for a moment, but she didn't answer, and Cathy knew that Alfie hadn't lied.

She slammed the door and ran upstairs, spreading out glass and shells under her bedside lamp, peering through tears until she found two nuggets of amber that were exactly the same colour. One was the shape of a 'fat sunflower seed, like a cat's half-closed eye; the other was only a slender shard. She wasn't sure whether that mattered, but she tucked them under her pillow anyway.

In her sleep, the cat came, half-hidden by the leaves of the laurel hedge, his grin as wide as a plate, and his stripes as fiercely orange and as densely black as a tiger's. She couldn't quite make out his eyes, yet she sensed there was something odd about them.

In the morning, Cathy took the bigger pieces of sea glass and slipped them into her blazer pocket, and on the way back from school she walked down Castlegate. She slowed down as she passed number seventeen, and threw the largest pebble as hard as she could at the parlour window. There was a loud crack, and when she looked over her shoulder, Cathy saw a woman peering out, her mouth wide in surprise. A man flung open the door, and she knew it was her da; she recognised him from the photographs Mam kept hidden at the back of the bureau. He shouted after her, cursing, as though she was another good-for-nothing school kid. A stranger. She ran home through the ginnels, beads of glass falling from her pockets and skittering across the cobbles.

When she passed Alfie's house, she noticed a tabby cat sitting on the garden wall. He weighed her up through one half-closed eye that was the colour of thick-cut marmalade. His other eye was sewn shut.

HORSES

The man and the woman arrived at the Gare du Nord on a Friday evening. Anyone who cared to observe them would have thought them an odd match. Hugh melted into the crowd and left no lasting impression in his wake. He was blond like Marielle, but they were two different kinds of pale. She was spun gold, radiating light, whereas he was a dull kind of fair, where hair, skin, and features blended into beige.

She strode ahead of him down the street, a bright bloom weaving through the crowds, leaving Hugh to carry her suitcase as he followed. She was scarcely aware that men stared at her, and although she knew that Hugh could not be considered handsome, it had never mattered.

The hotel he'd picked was a short walk from the station. The brochure showed a classic facade, an over-gilded rococo lounge, and an old-fashioned lift with iron gates. But the room they were given was small, dark, and womb-like, decorated in a deep crimson. The windows opened onto a crumbling balcony strewn with cigarette ends.

Marielle tried to hide her disappointment, but she'd looked forward to this visit to Paris for so long, and felt as though the hotel room was an inauspicious start. She ignored Hugh's suggestion that they should rest for an hour, and insisted that they freshened up and went straight out.

She said she was hungry, and they went back down the street to a bistro on the corner that offered a set price dinner. They ate inside, at a small booth in the window, and it was stuffy and warm even though it was cool outside. The food was mediocre: the bread was yesterday's and their omelettes were overcooked. She smiled, and said it was fine, and they both drank too much wine because they knew it wasn't.

As they waited for their dessert they watched a woman feeding pigeons from a bag of bread and cake crumbs. A group of teenagers turned into the street and the birds took flight in a whir of wings. One of the girls picked up a larger piece of the bread and threw it at the woman's head. It caught her off-balance and she staggered sideways. The girl's friends laughed. Encouraged, she picked up another piece and swung her arm back again. Marielle looked at Hugh, but he just shrugged and muttered that it was none of their business.

Marielle leapt to her feet and ran outside, screeching at the group like a fishwife. They moved off, laughing, shouting in French that she didn't understand as they disappeared down the street.

She came back inside and sat down, suddenly aware that she was shaking.

Hugh hardly glanced at her. He was looking around the room to deflect the amused stares of their fellow diners. She didn't know what he was thinking, but she knew that something had changed between them. For some reason she had been sure he would be proud of her for intervening, for helping. But instead he seemed embarrassed by her, and she was sad that he was no longer on her side.

They said nothing to each other of this bleak discovery,

but paid the bill and walked to the metro station to take a train for the Eiffel Tower, sitting in silence until they reached Champs de Mar. When they joined the queue for the tower, Marielle softened and took Hugh's arm, hoping it would be romantic when Paris was spread out beneath them in the dark, glittering like an open jewellery box.

Yet when they reached the platform it was crowded, filled with loud chatter and cameras flashing in every direction. Marielle looked down at the view and Hugh reached for her hand. This wasn't how she'd imagined it. She thought he would take her outside and wrap his coat around her, enveloping the two of them in their own secret world. She had felt sure that this moment would save them, but she could see now that it was a mistake. Why had she thought that Paris would be anything other than a cliché?

When they came back down they walked over to the crepe stall by the merry-go-round. They bought coffee and sat down on a nearby bench. The carousel was closed but the music still played on, and the cleaner was sweeping between the brightly coloured horses, her hair tucked inside a flowered turban. The tower still sparkled with a million lights and the carousel was a riot of red and gold. It was Marielle's Parisienne moment; the thing she would always remember. But it would be her memory alone. They had moved to a place where they would always be side by side, seeing the same things differently, instead of watching for the reflection of a place in the other's smile. She held the weight of this discovery inside her like a dull, heavy stone.

The next day they queued to see the *Mona Lisa* and, like all of Paris, it was less than Marielle had hoped for. She could scarcely see as people pressed all around her; the painting was so small, so distanced by the glass surrounding it. She wanted to walk back and forth across the floor, to see the eyes follow her as they were famed to do. But the crowds closed in behind them and so they went back out into the sun.

She knew that Hugh would visit Paris again. He would take his wife, and his son and daughter. They would go to a show, and he would watch dancing girls who - just for a moment - would make him think of Marielle. Then he would order champagne and chase her from his mind. And this would be how he would punish her, even though she wouldn't see it. He would do this until he had over-written the memories with something that made Paris good for him. But Marielle would still have her memory of the brightly coloured horses, and she didn't need Paris to be anything else.

They walked back through the streets side by side, both knowing that they had peeled back the dead layers of their affair and discovered its empty heart. They knew it was over, but each of them still said to the other how lovely it had been.

BETTER TO SEE HIM DEAD

I waited for the curtains to close around Mama's coffin. They stuttered for a moment as they jerked along the rails, the sound drowned out by the Buddy Holly song she'd chosen. Hearing that song was the saddest thing of all; it was my father's favourite, yet it had never been my mother's. Even in death she couldn't let him go.

I turned my head, and her sister, Jenny, caught my eye. We were silent allies, alone in our understanding of Mama's wasted life; and the knowing of it was a heavy thing to share. When we stepped outside, my uncle put his hand on my shoulder. He said he was sorry, and muttered the words he hoped were the good ones and the right ones. He knew, he said, that it must be really hard for me right now, what with Ged no longer being around.

I needed to avoid hearing the other words that might follow: the bad ones and the wrong ones, so I told my uncle I'd meet up with the family later, at the bar on the corner of Union. Then I headed down Kingsway to the beach.

A sharp wind raced in from the sea, and an empty soda

bottle skittered along the boardwalk above me, clattering against the railings. I stumbled against something in the sand; the rotting remains of a gull, bloodied and flattened, one rheumy eye staring up at me.

As I climbed back up the steps, I saw a figure move towards the door in the fortune-teller's booth. The lights flickered on and off around the sign. She beckoned, and in the fast-fading dusk her eyes were as blank as the dead bird's. I strode straight past, and she called after me as I walked away, but I didn't turn round. I knew she couldn't see into my future, but there was a chance that she would see straight into my past.

Way back when, the booth had belonged to Madame Rosa. She advertised herself as a true Romany, with a gift for palmistry and crystal-gazing that had been passed down through generations. Yet everyone knew that her mother was one of the Elwood Park Bradshaws, and that she had been married to a vacuum cleaner salesman from Seattle.

In the school holidays, Mama used to take me with her to the booth sometimes. I would perch on the velvet seat at the back while Rosa ran her claw-like nails along the lines in my mother's palm, telling her everything she wanted to hear about the love and money that were sure to be coming her way real soon.

One time, she called me over to have my palm read too. I hesitated, but Mama pushed me forward and thrust my nail-bitten hand across the table. Madame Rosa leaned in close, and I could see her blue eyeshadow caked in the creases, and the feathery lines of lipstick that bled from her mouth. She told me that when I grew up I'd be just like my mother, and I snatched my hand back and shook my head.

'I don't want to be like her,' I whispered. 'Mama wishes

my daddy was dead. She says better to see him dead than to let him love another woman.'

That was when Mama grabbed my hand and twisted me round, almost lifting me off the floor as she pulled me back out of the booth. I still remember the knowing smile of Madame Rosa, and the shrill laughter that followed us down the boardwalk.

***

The summer I met Ged, I was just seventeen. Every day, I sat on the porch and watched the tarmac shimmer with mirages, conjuring and re-conjuring his shape out of the haze as I waited patiently for him to ride up the street.

Mama stayed inside, out of the sun, standing at the window in her stained satin slip. Sometimes she walked from room to room, opening and closing the drawers and cupboards as though searching for something to help her make sense of the world. She was still saying that she'd rather see my father dead than out in that world with someone else, and I still asked her not to talk that way.

In the years since he'd gone, I hadn't seen my daddy much at all, yet sometimes his absence slammed into me as though he'd left only yesterday. He'd moved out to live with one of his girlfriends in a trailer park a few miles west of Madeley, and it was a good three hours each way on the bus if I wanted to make the trip to see him. For the most part, I replayed my memories instead. I remembered the trips to the boardwalk on a Sunday morning, sitting alongside him at the diner counter and ordering a stack of pancakes. He didn't talk much, but he watched me eat those pancakes drenched with syrup, and smiled and nodded as though I'd done something to make him proud. And I remember the beautiful kite we flew; a white eagle that soared and dived above the pale sand. On the way home we would listen to the rock and roll station on the radio, and Daddy would sing along to Buddy Holly. When we got back, Mama would run down the porch steps to greet us, smelling of her special perfume that was as dark and musty as the forest floor. She would take my father's hand and they would walk inside together in silence. Over lunch I would tell Mama all about our morning, but Daddy rarely said a word.

Ged was a lot like my father. He didn't say much, and I never minded. He talked with his eyes and his hands, and I knew he loved me.

When I lay awake late at night, I listened out for his motorbike, and his quiet footsteps on the porch before he tapped on the glass. I would lift the sash and he would climb over the sill and kick off his boots. He would hold me tightly, as though he could disappear by becoming part of me, his leather jacket cool and smooth against my cheek. I left the light out, so we didn't have to look into each other's eyes. I told him it was so we didn't wake Mama, but the truth was that I was scared to see too much, and to face the fact that there was no return, or maybe to see too little, and to discover that what I thought was real was something else.

I would kiss him through the open window as he left, reluctant to let him go. Sometimes, on a hot night, I would step out onto the porch with him. He would press me against the wall and we would slide slowly to the floor, to the still-warm wood. He would spread out his leather jacket beneath me, and I would look at him then, in the cold, silver light. The fear of losing him matched the joy of the moment. He would sense it and shiver, pull on his jeans, and leave without a word.

***

When we moved in together, we left town and rented a house by Edgewood Lake. Ged got a job on Bleecker's Farm, and we were happy for a while.

But it wasn't long before he started to pace the house like a caged coyote. A mask of silent anger would darken his face for days at a time. When he came home from the farm he would take a cold beer from the fridge and sit at the kitchen table staring at the wall. We no longer went down to the shore or hung out with our friends along the boardwalk.

One time, I took his lunch across to the farm. I could see the tractor at the far side of the field, and the newly ploughed furrows that stretched away to the edge of the pine woods. I waved as I walked towards him, but the sun reflected off his windscreen and I couldn't tell if he waved back. As he got nearer I held up the rucksack. He stopped, and jumped down, and I handed over the soup and sandwiches. He didn't make eye contact, but simply nodded and walked back to the tractor, leaping up in one easy stride. It was cold, but I didn't move. I watched him driving up and down the field, turning the earth, and I had no idea what to do to make it better.

Then Nelson arrived.

Ged wasn't fond of cats, yet he took to this tiny stray with the missing eye; the other the same bright blue as his own. Nelson was our charm, and I prayed for us.

We got caught in a downpour one afternoon as we were gathering firewood, and we raced back to the house, laughing as we slid in the mud. It was a rare good day; Ged seemed happy.

I threw our muddy clothes in the washing machine while he heated some soup. We sat down to eat and I asked if he'd seen Nelson. The cat had been asleep by the stove when we walked in, but now he'd disappeared. It wasn't like him to go out in the rain. Our eyes met, and we both jumped up. Nelson was always climbing into the washer. I ran through to the machine and saw his tiny body turning with the clothes. I hit the stop button, but I couldn't bear to look again and see him limp and still.

Ged peered into the drum. 'It's ok,' he said, 'he's still moving.'

We wrapped him in a towel and he fell asleep in the crook of Ged's arm.

Later, we made love for the first time in months. The rain had stopped, and through the open window I heard the low, quavering hoot of an owl. Nelson's tiny head lifted for a moment before he curled round asleep again.

I watched their faces as they slept. We were all safe.

But the next day Ged's eyes looked straight through me. I made pancakes for breakfast, but he said he was going into town. Nelson slipped out of the door behind him. I stood at the window like my mother used to do, waiting for them both to come back.

***

Two months later, Ged didn't come home one night after work. I sat in the porch chair to wait for him, listening to the night noise: the laughter and shrieks, the car horns and sirens, music from a window across the street, the dull thrum of lorries on the distant freeway. But all the time I was listening for Ged's motorbike, and I was counting, slowly. He would be home by the time I had counted to a hundred. Two hundred. Or when twenty cars had gone past the end of the street. Thirty.

I was woken the next morning by a tapping sound: a key against glass. I jumped up and went into the living room, flinching when I threw back the curtains and the sunlight flooded in.

Maggie, the local deputy, stood at the door, her hand cupped against the window.

Ged had taken a bend too fast, hit the barrier, and then the windscreen of a pick-up truck.

And as she guided me to the kitchen table, I saw it: the truth. I understood the worst of myself for the first time; the relief pushing out the fear, and the new understanding of how things could be. This way Ged could never leave me, and I would never become my mother.

It was the best way to end it, just like Mama always said.

When I followed Maggie to the car I noticed a dead mouse stretched out across the porch step. I guess it was a gift from Nelson, but from that day on, I never saw him again.

WHATEVER SPEED SHE DARED

The rear lights of the cars ahead disappear one by one over the horizon. There are no approaching headlamps, and nothing behind. The empty motorway is all hers, carving its way west through the peat-bleak moorland.

Right now, she could drive in whichever lane she wanted at whatever speed she dared. She could criss-cross the curving lines of cats' eyes, veer from the hard shoulder to the central barrier and back again, wind down the window, blast out 'Born to Run', howl into the night like an American werewolf.

She feels light-headed, and in a rare moment of clarity she glimpses her future; a new knowing of how it will be. Now that she's found the courage to leave Carl, she's sure she has the strength to make it good.

Caught in her main beam, a skittish rabbit makes a bid for the other side. He pauses for a moment, gold-flecked fur and liquid eyes, his ears raised, one front paw held high. She lifts her own foot off the accelerator, and grips the wheel, ready to brake. But the rabbit moves off again at a measured pace, unhurried but purposeful, leaping over the barrier and melting into the darkness. She imagines the bob of his tail disappearing beneath the dank earth into a warren filled with half-blind kittens; a sudden reminder that the body of a murdered child still lies undiscovered on this moor, buried in the sodden peat.

Her new-found courage falters, and she thinks that perhaps she should give Carl another chance. She shivers and turns the music down, then moves over to the inside lane, reducing her speed until headlights appear in her rear-view mirror again. As she approaches the next junction she reads the road signs. Carl will be home from the pub now, he'll already be wondering where she is. If she turns round here she can be back in an hour. She could call and tell him she finished her shift late, and that she'll stop off for a takeaway.

As she indicates to leave the motorway, a shooting star arcs across the sky. She gasps, and then remembers hearing it on the news earlier - tonight is the best night of the year for seeing the Perseid meteor shower. She takes the exit, but she doesn't turn for home. Instead she follows the B road that takes her high up onto the moors, above the ambient light of the motorway. She parks and gets out, then lays down in the heather to watch the stars; dense handfuls filling every inch of sky. So many stars on which to hang a wish.

When she gets back in the car she knows what to do. She'll go home, and tell Carl she's leaving. She'll explain it to him, face to face, and she won't let him change her mind. Because daring isn't about running away in the dark; it's about walking away in plain sight, without once looking back.

ALREADY FORMED

Every August my summer boy arrived on the beach. I watched him from my studio window, and sometimes I made sketches of him; a boy created in the image of Rory, caramel-skinned and lathe-thin, like a shaft of sunlight.

I often saw him when I went for my morning walk. A line of upturned rowboats basked in the dunes like a row of giant turtles, and he would slalom between them as he raced down to the receding shoreline.

On my return I'd find him crouched over rock pools, parting fronds of seaweed to reveal tiny crabs, his slender fingers entwined with the blood-red tentacles of sea anemones. At his side there would be a bucket filled with shells and freckled pebbles, their colours fading to pale as they dried in the sun.

And as I watched him, I imagined he was Rory, separated from me at birth by a mistake, waiting for me to reclaim him when the moment was right. We'd build sandcastles decorated with shells, win Love Hearts and key rings on the penny falls, then walk down to Balducci's for ice cream sodas.

It was difficult to remember my life before Rory. He became mortal even before I did the pregnancy test. He was already part of everything; as tangible as if he'd already been born. He was your reassurance that you wouldn't let me down, that you'd finally tell your wife about us. The day I did the test you bought me the sea-green dress that shimmered, and you told me I was your mermaid. And Rory was the sound of my laugh when I threw the shopping bag onto the bed, reminding you that in a few months' time I may be too big to wear it. At that moment Rory became the inevitable future: just me, a baby, and a life filled with bottles and nappies. And occasionally there'd be you. But in that vision the sea was always rough, and I couldn't see the horizon for rain on the glass.

Finally he was my forehead against the cool bathroom tiles, and the knot in my stomach as I waited for the line to turn blue. And then, just like that, he was gone. Gone without touching the sides. Rory wasn't even a blue line on a pregnancy test. He was a line missing. He was your obvious relief, your pale smile, your cold fingers on my arm. He was your voice telling me that you would have been torn between this new baby and your own children. You didn't say your other children, but your own children. As though Rory would have been less yours in some way. And as I lay awake that night, my relief changed to grief. I grieved for the inevitable end of our affair, and for the loss of the unwanted child who was already formed in my mind.

In the holidays I still went down to my beach house to paint, half-hoping, half-dreading that you'd arrive next door just as before. You'd always used your cottage as a refuge, a place you could work in peace - no wife, no teenagers home from college, no computer games blaring. But for months on end it stood empty, the shutters battened and peeling. The following summer I heard a rumour that you'd moved to London, and so I guessed you were never coming back.

The whole of July was cool and cloudy, and I became

restless. Then on the first Saturday in August a dented blue Land Rover pulled up outside, and I rushed straight to the window to assess the new tenant. A woman was lifting a baby carrier from the front seat, and as she walked over to the cottage the sun appeared, exactly as though it had been waiting for their arrival. She stopped for a moment to scan the horizon, holding a hand up to shield her eyes before going inside to throw open the shutters.

She had brought my summer boy, and I no longer needed to think about you. I had Rory instead.

That first year I watched him in the cottage garden, never out of his mother's sight. When I saw them getting ready for their walk I would rush outside, clutching my trowel and secateurs. The woman hardly noticed me as they passed by, the pram dusted in fine, pale sand, and Rory dressed in tiny sleep suits patterned with red and blue yachts, his hair a handful of spun gold.

I was pleased that she paid me no attention, for if we had introduced ourselves I would have found out the boy's name too, and if he became Joshua or Harry or Tom, then he could no longer be Rory.

The following year I watched him take his first tentative steps. And as soon as he could walk he found the sea. Whenever his mother dragged him back he would spin straight round and waddle to the water's edge again. He flicked up seaweed with his neon-pink spade, giggling with glee at the stub-legged dachshund that circled him.

When he was old enough to explore by himself he conquered the beach: no stone unturned, no dune uncharted. His strong limbs carried him across the sand, fishnet trailing, tongue curled around his upper lip in concentration as he picked up starfish and hermit crabs, and cautiously touched jellyfish with the tip of his rubber flip flops. His mother would leave him to play for hours on end whilst she sunbathed or read her book.

I could never understand why she didn't want to watch him every minute of the day as I did, trailing in his footsteps, mesmerised by each perfect bare footprint, each sandcastle, each shriek of joy.

One afternoon, in Rory's seventh summer, I saw him stretched out on the edge of the slipway after a swim, his eyes closed against the sun. I wanted to touch his hair, his long pale lashes, to smell the summer heat and the sea salt on his skin. I walked on the beach at the side of the slipway, my face level with his, and stopped to watch him. I reached out my hand to stroke the smooth skin on his cheek. As my fingers hovered above his face, he opened his eyes. As he met my gaze, I was transfixed, not noticing his mother until she started to run towards us. I pulled my sunhat down over my eyes, left the beach quickly without looking back.

I went straight to the house and up to my studio. I filled sheet after sheet of paper with bold strokes of colour, tacking them randomly to the wall behind me. I needed to capture Rory's essence, to feel his movements through my pencil and my brush. He was the colours of the dunes: the sand, the wild flowers and the wind-blown couch grass. He was the colours of the sea: the water and the white spume beneath the unbroken blue of the sky. And more than all of those he was the colours of the rock pools: the reds, the greens, the speckled browns and pinks.

And for the first time in months, I thought of you. Where were you now? Did you ever wonder how lonely I might be? Did you assume I'd be with someone else, never imagining that I'd be tied to the past, to the memories of our last day, to the son I had created in my mind?

I found the white carrier bag that had remained untouched at the back of the wardrobe and took out the mermaid dress. It shimmered in the sun as I shook the dust from its folds and stepped into it. It still fitted; a sheath of iridescent scales.

When I heard someone knocking, for a moment I imagined it was you, and that I'd conjured you by thought. I rushed downstairs, running my fingers through my hair and straightening the dress, calling out to you. There were two policemen stood at the door, and stupidly I thought they had brought news of you. I probably sounded nervous when I asked them what they wanted. The younger one touched the front of his cap respectfully, and said they were sorry to bother me, that they could see I was busy. I must have looked questioningly at him, because he gestured to my hands, to the smears of yellow ochre and cerulean blue. My hands were daubed with the colours of my summer boy.

The policeman was saying something about a woman; a woman with a red sunhat who was seen by the slipway. There'd been a complaint. A mother, her young boy, my neighbours. Did I know them? Had I seen anyone hanging around the beach? I shook my head and muttered a reply.

As they walked back down the path I snatched my sunhat from the window ledge and pushed it down the side of the chair. The mermaid dress was now smeared with paint and the sky had clouded over.

The next day I bought a new hat from the souvenir shop, then took a walk towards the village. It was as I climbed the steps near the pier that I saw you. You were sat in a car at the traffic lights on the shore road, heading towards the cottages. You didn't see me, you were too intent on the road. You looked worried, older, your hair shot with grey, and I knew for certain that you weren't looking for me.

I ran back along the beach, and when I saw the car parked outside your cottage, I understood. What I had seen in the boy's face was you, and somewhere within me I had known this from the start. Because all along you had your own Rory, already formed, already growing, already more than a blue line.

You knocked on my door before you left, and I let you in without saying a word. I knew you'd already have guessed that I was the woman on the beach - it was you who bought me the red hat. But neither of us spoke of it.

'Did you know your wife was pregnant when I did the test?' I asked.

You nodded, but you didn't say you were sorry.

'I've been working away a lot these last few years,' you said. 'London, Brussels, New York.'

When you left, I followed you to the door, and watched you drive away. I hadn't told you that I didn't realise the woman was your wife, or that the boy was your son. It would have sounded too incredible.

For the next few years I still saw them both when they came to the house for those three weeks in August. When I bumped into your wife in the village shop, or we passed on the beach path, I sometimes said hello. She always looked puzzled, as though she could never quite place me, and then she would instinctively reach for my summer boy's hand.

THE LAST OF MICHIKO

Hitoshi knelt on a blue cushion in the doorway leading out to the garden. Every evening he opened the outer doors and the sliding screens regardless of the season, and waited for Michiko until long after the sun had disappeared behind the trees. His heart knew that she would never return, but his head was stubborn.

The windchimes jingled in the sudden breeze, mimicking Michiko's laugh, and Hitoshi pressed his face into her pink kimono, inhaling the amber scent. At his side stood a jar of her homemade adzuki jam, as sweet and red as her lips. He had rationed it carefully, but the jar was almost empty.

The day's post was propped up against the screen, and Hitoshi reached for the bills and the letter from his daughter. She wrote each week and always asked him to stay with her for a while. Sometimes he thought he would go, but the trip to Tokyo seemed like such a long journey now, and the city blinded him. There were no distances; everything was too densely packed, too close to see. And what about Michiko? He couldn't risk her returning to the empty house in his absence.

His son, Shoichi, lived nearer, but when Hitoshi saw the car pull up he stayed out of sight and didn't answer the door.

He couldn't face the words that needed to be said, and he couldn't bear to be reminded of the dark water snatching Michiko away as though she were a brittle twig. When Hitoshi thought of that day he pictured her hair floating upwards like the darkest seaweed, her skin as cold and blue as the sea, and though he knew he should talk to his son, he couldn't face hearing Shoichi say that he was sure his mother had drowned.

Some evenings Hitoshi thought he heard a faint knocking at the door, but when he went outside, the narrow street was always empty. He stayed there awhile, peering into the darkness, his mind tricking him into hearing Michiko's wooden clogs on the cobbles. In the distance he glimpsed the soft light of the lantern outside the izakaya. He imagined the warmth inside, the kind face of Kyoko as she poured the sake, and his friend, Wada, sat at the counter waiting to mull over the latest baseball game. But Hitoshi always went back into the house and sat alone again in the dark.

Tonight there was no knocking, but just after seven o'clock the doorbell rang. When he opened the screen he saw his neighbour, the young widow, Chiyoko, stood beneath the light cradling a jar in both hands.

'I found this in the cupboard, Hitoshi-san. It's the last of Michiko's sweet bean jam.'

As he took the jar, Hitoshi stumbled under the weight of its significance. He looked up at Chiyoko as she discreetly backed away, and when their eyes met she paused. He bowed, and gestured her inside, apologising for his rudeness. She slipped off her shoes and stepped past him, her kimono sweeping the tatami floor like a new broom. As the door closed, Hitoshi noticed that Michiko's wind chimes had fallen silent.

***

As the weeks went by Hitoshi found himself looking forward to Chiyoko's visits more and more. He was calmed by her gentle movements as she prepared tea or served warmed sake on a lacquer tray. Her conversation was undemanding, and her voice soothed him as she chatted about the neighbourhood and her office job in town. They rarely mentioned Michiko, but she often pressed him to talk about his children, persuading him to ask them both over for a family weekend.

Chiyoko was quite similar to his wife in appearance, and at first Hitoshi had found himself continually staring at her, searching her face for everything he had lost. She always changed out of her work suit before she visited, and the soft colours and patterns of her kimonos were a further reminder of his wife. Occasionally, when he'd caught a glimpse of her heavy silk sleeve around the edge of the door, he had been certain for a moment that Michiko would walk into the room.

While Chiyoko talked to him, he always sat facing the garden, the screens open, looking out through the glass of the outer doors. And when she went home he moved to his cushion in the doorway and let the warm evening air into the house. It was only then that he could hear the wind chimes. The final jar of bean paste was always beside him, and each evening he tasted Michiko's lips on his own as he ate a single spoonful.

One evening Chiyoko noticed the jar on the floor and commented that there was only a teaspoon left. Hitoshi's reply was terse; he was only too aware of the significance of that one last mouthful of sweetness. Even the scent of Michiko's kimono was growing fainter, as though he had inhaled and absorbed every last thread and breath of her. When Chiyoko left, Hitoshi wept for the first time in months. The sound of his sobbing carried across the garden, and a dog howled in reply from the valley beyond.

***

The following evening, Chiyoko called at the usual time, holding up a jar of bean jam at the window. She claimed that she found it tucked away at the back of another cupboard. Hitoshi took it from her, holding it up to the light. The screw top was green, and the jar angular. Hitoshi recognised it as a type of pickle jar, a brand that he and Michiko had never eaten. And the paste was too dark. He knew it was not Michiko's; he knew it was a deception. But he understood it was meant as a kind one.

After Chiyoko had gone home he sat in the doorway watching the fireflies for a while, then fetched a pen and paper and wrote a short note asking her to lunch at the weekend to meet his son and daughter.

When he dropped it through her door he glanced along the street towards the izakaya, wondering if Wada would be there at his usual place at the counter. Chiyoko had told him that Wada and Kyoko were finally a couple after all their years of shy flirtation, and the thought of them together made him smile. The red lantern swayed in the soft evening breeze as though beckoning him. Hitoshi counted the loose change in his pocket to make sure he had enough money for a couple of beers, and then he headed down the street.

ALL STATIONS TO EDGWARE

As she walked through the tunnel towards the platform, Eleanor felt a sudden blast of stale breath from the mouth of an approaching train. She found it oddly comforting. The Tube seemed much the same as when she had last lived in London in 1972.

She checked her piece of paper to make sure she was heading in the right direction. On the platform, she looked up at the electronic screen. The next train was due in two minutes, for all stations to Edgware.

There were still a few seats, and Eleanor flopped down, dragging her bag awkwardly behind her. She always managed to take up more space than anyone else. She moved carelessly and extravagantly, sweeping papers onto the floor with a kimono sleeve or trailing the hem of her long cotton dress in the damp Indian earth. Even here, in the crowded train, she was sprawled across two seats, her rucksack on the verge of toppling into someone's lap. Despite the fact that she was going to the end of the line, she still checked the LED indicator as the train pulled into each station.

Euston. As the train stopped, a woman pushed past her towards the door, and Eleanor caught the earthy scent of patchouli. She could feel the warmth of the soft Jaipur dusk, the air heavy with incense and sandalwood attar, saris catching the light, and silk scarves billowing like jewel-bright parachutes.

The bride, nervous and pale, had been beautifully gift-wrapped in red and gold. Eleanor dipped her thumb into a silver dish of kumkum powder and rose petals, pressing it gently to the girl's forehead as she wished her luck. Anish had been the only friend she had left in India, and at his wedding he had been taken from her by a shy temptress and family tradition.

Mornington Crescent. Eleanor thought of her mother listening to *I'm Sorry I Haven't a Clue*. Sometimes, when she was homesick, she had listened to it herself on the World Service. There was a certain short-lived comfort in hearing the measured tones of a BBC voice, in thinking that her mother may be listening, and laughing, at the unmistakably British humour. But in the end, she stopped. It only made her feel farther away, and at the same time it reminded her of why she had left.

Camden Town. The train emptied and waited quietly on the platform. She caught sight of her reflection in the window. Frayed at the edges, on the brink of old age, a face reddened and coarsened by too many days in the sun and too many bottles of cheap whisky.

As the doors closed, a young woman jumped on, olive-skinned, with eyes of bitter chocolate. Eleanor felt the thick heat of the market in Mapusa, and saw the two couples in the bar. It was late morning and she was already adding whisky to her soda.

The girls had been shopping in the market, laughing and joking, showing the men the scarves and spices they had bought. The girl with the dark hair was striking. A streak of jealousy flashed through Eleanor, a desperate longing for the beauty and chances she had lost. Fuelled by whisky, she flirted outrageously with the men; a lush in a faded dress. She heard the girls laughing at her, and spat and hissed at them like a cat, until Vinod told her to go home.

India had made her unbearably tired of herself. Each summer she prayed for the monsoon to come early, and for an end to the oppressive heat. Then she would pray for an end to the relentless rain, and after the rain she was grateful for the lull, and the warm, musty damp.

Chalk Farm. A couple sat down, chatting animatedly in French. As their voices washed over her, Eleanor could almost taste the dank, pulsing heat of the club in Paris. Her fixed smile had never slipped as she danced, and as she sat in the laps of leering drunks. It was cramped, dark, filled with tobacco smoke, and the reek of cheap powder and sweat. She had shared a dressing room with six other girls. Occasionally, one of them would disappear and be replaced without a word. She guessed where they went, she had seen the rich Arab clientele watching them dance, eyeing up the next recruits for their floating harems.

She started drinking whisky before she went on stage, just to take the edge off. One night, she tripped in the alleyway as she staggered out of the stage door. A man reached out for her hand and pulled her to her feet. Then he stepped back, bowed, and handed her a business card. He asked if she would come to Japan and work as the chief hostess in his club in Tokyo. He said he had been watching her.

Akiro had rescued her, just as a European in Japan might have fallen in love with a geisha from the tea house and taken her back to his bland apartment in a western city. And ever after, when she heard the sound of tea pouring, she would recall the fresh hay scent of a tatami floor and dream of Kyoto. Eleanor smelt the tatami and thought of heather on the Yorkshire moors, blazing purple as far as the eye could see, punctuated by the tiny dots of grazing sheep.

Hampstead. Eleanor was jerked awake as the train juddered to a halt. She had fallen asleep and missed Belsize Park. A fragment of her dream stayed with her for a moment, and she imagined she could see Jay further down the platform, walking away from her. She half-stood in her seat, almost called out his name, craning to see him as he disappeared from view, his hair just touching the collar of his denim shirt, his desert boots scuffed and stained. She remembered his wide smile when she agreed to move to London with him. Two shy teenagers, blinded by the bright certainty of their love.

She wondered if Suzie still lived in Hampstead. How could she have lost touch with her oldest friend? She had written to Eleanor in Paris and through all the years in Tokyo. She let her know that Jay was in India, and helped her to track him down, even though it had proved too late for forgiveness. And Suzie had never mentioned Vinnie. There was no reproach, she had never asked why Eleanor had done the unthinkable thing. Suzie had not judged her for leaving her own son behind.

Golders Green. As the doors slid open like paper shoji screens, sunshine flooded into the carriage. Akiro would open the screens onto the balcony at the first sign of spring, and gaze across the trees at the mountains, still topped with snow. He would sit on a red cushion and write in his journal. The scratch of the ink pen on the rough paper made her think of her father, head bent over his desk in the study. She would peer round the door and watch him silently. Yet he always knew she was there, and just when she least expected it, he would turn to her and smile.

Brent Cross. Two young women struggled onto the train with shopping and a buggy. They laughed and chatted, and the boy sat quietly. Not like Vinnie.

Jay had been wonderful with Vinnie. Eleanor had felt stifled and constricted, sometimes every breath was an effort. She would take him with her to dance classes, and Suzie would keep him entertained. Yet at nearly every class Suzie would be forced to interrupt, as Vinnie would scream for her, for something she didn't know how to give.

She had never been one to do what was expected, so no one was surprised when she booked a flight to Paris and left a note on the kitchen table.

Hendon. From the train she could see neat suburban houses with their dull, manicured gardens. Jay and Eleanor had always hated houses like these. They promised each other that their garden would be a riot of colour and mayhem.

Colindale. There was a story on the news about Colindale the night before. She watched it on the television in her hotel room. A woman was found dead in her flat, six whole weeks after she died. The neighbours only called the police when they saw swarms of flies coming out of her open kitchen window. There were sixteen bottles of milk outside the door. Two weeks and two days before the milkman gave up. Even then, he didn't report anything amiss. Eleanor took note of the story because the woman was her own age.

Burnt Oak. Eleanor thought of Jay sat beneath the huge oak in Tofts Meadow, leaning back against the rough bark, eyes closed, long lashes almost touching his cheeks. They would ride out there on his motorbike, carrying her mother's old plaid rug, squashed cucumber sandwiches, and a bottle of warm, too-sweet wine that they had stolen from her father's cellar. She cartwheeled around the field and told Jay that one day she would dance at the Moulin Rouge.

Sweet, gentle Jay, the father of her son. Her son, Vinnie, who despite everything had tracked her down, sent her a plane ticket and offered her a home. The prodigal mother returning to the fold. She touched the hip flask in her pocket.

Edgware. Outside Edgware station she gave Vinnie's address to the cab driver. They turned into a street lined with cherry trees, the pavement strewn with drifts of pink petals. Eleanor felt the soft, sweet breath of spring touching the heavy boughs of blossom by the bridge in Tokyo. She could see the lanterns outside the tea houses, hear the crunch of gravel on the temple path.

The taxi pulled up; the end of yet another journey. All this running, and yet she had never managed to escape herself or find herself. A life of hide and seek. And in the end it was all the same. You knew what you'd always known: that wherever you go, there you are.

Eleanor peered out at the house. Was this to be the end of all her journeys? This neatly trimmed garden in suburban London, this mocking mock-Tudor in earshot of the tired drone of the M1. Brightly painted gnomes were lined up at the side of the driveway, and she saw a woman in the window, her neck held taut in the manner of a disapproving tortoise.

A man walked down the street towards her, briefcase in hand, prematurely grey, hunched with disappointment. He turned in at the gate of number forty-three and her heart stopped. Vinnie. He paused, and bent down to pull up a lone yellow wallflower that had dared to grow in a crack in the

71

driveway. Eleanor waited to see if he would hold the flower up to his nose and inhale the heady scent, but he lifted the lid of the wheelie bin and dropped it inside.

She leant forward towards the cab driver and tapped the glass screen.

THE SHADOW
ARCHITECT

Satseko flipped open the postbox and retrieved a battered postcard that looked as though it had travelled twice round the world to find her. She picked up her grocery bags and walked over to the lift as she examined the picture. It was a reproduction of an old woodblock print, just like the postcards that her mother, Natsuko, had kept in the drawer of the dining room chest. She turned it over as she stepped into the lift, half-hoping that by some miracle her mother had sent it; that the clock had been turned back nine months and both her parents were still alive.

The card was postmarked Onokatsu, and was from Aunt Fumiko.

Don't worry about me, I'm doing fine. Reluctant to leave the village until the weather improves!

She sighed and pushed it into the top of her bag as she fished for her keys. She had invited her aunt to stay with her in Tokyo at least a dozen times since her parents' accident. The weather was a poor excuse. It was spring now, and the trees were already budding with blossom. She had imagined them walking to view the cherry trees on Shinjuku Gyoen, taking food and sake, sitting on the same picnic rug they had used when she was a child. The annual trip to Tokyo had always seemed exciting and exotic to Satseko: the neon-bright city, the novelty of staying with her grandparents in their modern apartment, and the fragile beauty of the cherry blossom.

When she finished college, Satseko moved to Tokyo for work, but her mother had always worried about her, convinced that the city was a dangerous place. She sent her a tiny wooden netsuke figure to which she'd attached homemade paper wings, and told her daughter to look upon it as her guardian angel.

As she opened the apartment door, Akira Okada walked past, hunched inside his coat. He had lived there just a matter of months, but there was a comforting familiarity about him. As usual he didn't look up, but just waved a hand when she called out a greeting. Despite the fact that he was a man of few words, he would sometimes leave a gift of food outside her door - a bag of tiny cakes, or a jar of pickled plums. He always rang the bell, but by the time she answered he had already walked away, and she would glimpse only his shadow as he turned the corner. Occasionally he would push a postcard underneath the door warning her of a typhoon forecast, or an envelope enclosing a discount coupon for the corner supermarket. Satseko wished she could tell her mother about him; it was almost as though he had been sent as the very guardian angel Natsuko had wanted for her.

She had asked the neighbours about Akira Okada, but no one seemed to know any details, only that he was retired and came from a small village near Kobe. When Satseko mentioned his wife - a woman she only saw fleetingly through the window - her neighbours seemed surprised, as they had heard he was a widower. She was puzzled. The woman definitely existed, but it would appear no one had ever seen her outside the apartment. She considered the possibility that she could be housebound, but this seemed unlikely, because every evening Satseko watched her dance.

The windows of the Okadas' apartment looked into the well of the building, at right angles to hers. They often left the shoji screens half-open after they'd turned on the lamps, and every evening shadows flitted across the paper panels as the couple danced. Satseko occasionally caught glimpses of Mrs Okada's yellow ball gown as they stepped out across the floor. Their silhouettes lengthened and shortened as they glided around the room like puppets in an ancient lantern theatre. As they moved close to the window she would see the distorted shadows of their faces on the panels of the screen, heads thrown back, paused as though waiting for applause before commencing the next dance.

As she put away her groceries Satseko glanced across at their apartment, but the room was in darkness.

When she had first seen the Okadas dancing, she had opened her window to try and listen to the music, but they had moved there in the autumn and the windows were usually closed in the evenings. Now it was warmer they were often thrown wide, but she no longer tried to listen, as she had made up her own mind which songs they played, and she sang them to herself as she watched. She imagined them dancing to Frank Sinatra and Dean Martin, just as her parents used to do when she was a child. Her mother had only ever had one interest: a passion for ballroom dancing. After each class she would teach her father the new steps she had learnt that evening. When she entered the house she would call out to him, breathless, as though she had run all the way home for fear of forgetting the new dance before she had the chance to show him.

'Kazuo, come quickly, I have some new steps to teach you!'

He would rush through to the hallway to help her out of her coat. The paperwork he had brought home from the bank would be forgotten, the ledgers left open on his desk, and his wire-rimmed reading glasses hurriedly removed.

Satseko would watch quietly in the corner, in awe of her mother as she crossed the room. She appeared elegant and a little distant; no longer the homely wife in a faded kimono. Her father would stumble and hesitate over the steps at first, but Natsuko was never impatient with him, and he looked into her eyes with devotion as they danced slow-slow-quick-quick-slow across the polished floor. His devotion made Satseko slightly sad, as even as a child she could see that her mother didn't feel the same. When she was a teenager Natsuko had told her that she'd married Kazuo because she was pregnant: that she'd had no choice. She joked that Satseko was a changeling, resembling neither of them, and then hugged her and laughed when she saw she was upset.

Satseko suddenly realised she was standing stock still, holding a box of rice in her hands as she stared out of the window. She opened the next cupboard and carried on putting her groceries away, turning on the radio to cut through the empty silence.

***

The following morning she called for an ambulance. The Okadas' rooms had remained in darkness the previous evening, and at first light she woke to hear a faint tapping through the party wall. She pulled on her clothes and rushed round to their door, but there was no answer.

The paramedics rang Satseko's bell when they arrived, and she took them across to the apartment. They hammered on the door, but there was only silence, and eventually they called the building manager for a key. Satseko hesitated on the doorstep, but the two men pushed her gently inside as they headed for the bedroom. She stood immobile just inside the entranceway, surrounded by walls filled with dance photographs, and a high shelf lined with trophies and rosettes.

The medics talked quietly and urgently from inside the bedroom. She heard the clang of apparatus before one of them rushed past her to fetch the stretcher from the corridor.

'Are they ok?' she asked.

'They? There's only the gentleman - he's suffered a severe cardiac arrest. Excuse me...'

Satseko stepped to one side, and when they walked back through with the laden stretcher she looked away, anxious not to see Akira's face.

'But his wife?' she asked.

They shrugged. 'There's no one else here. Will you be locking up?'

She nodded, watched them carry the stretcher awkwardly round the corner to the lift. She looked down at the key in her hand and then pushed the door open again, stepping quietly inside like a thief.

The living room was sparsely furnished and the chairs had been pushed to the edges of the room so that there was space to dance. She walked across to the window and slid back the screens to let in the light. When she turned away she saw a wooden mannequin slumped against the wall in the alcove: a woman in a yellow dress, one arm twisted at an awkward angle behind her, net underskirts spread out in a lake of pale sunshine. Mrs Okada was merely a life-size puppet, and Akira Okada was nothing more than a shadow architect.

Satseko didn't question why he would dance with a mannequin. Instead she was consumed by the irrational feeling that she had been cheated and deceived.

She went back into the hall and as she reached for the light switch in the entranceway she noticed that one of the photographs above was entitled 'Intermediate Class, Onokatsu'. Her heart flipped at the coincidence. She fetched a stool from the kitchen so that she could lift it down.

Her mother was on the front row, that unmistakable shy smile lighting up her face, wearing a yellow dress Satseko couldn't ever remember seeing. Something made her go back into the living room and look closely at a photograph in the alcove. It was Natsuko, wearing the same dress, the mannequin's dress, dancing with Akira Okada. They were on the dance floor alone, and there was an audience behind them, slightly out of focus. It looked as though they were taking part in a competition or show, but there was something unnervingly intimate about the way they held each other's gaze. Satseko's hand shook as she reached out to touch her mother's cheek. It was incredible and strange to think of her smile lighting up a room in a Tokyo apartment just yards from her own.

She looked more closely at Akira's face, and suddenly understood why he seemed oddly familiar: he had been Natsuko's dance teacher. When she was a child he often gave them a lift home if he chanced upon them in the town. She had always been a little scared of him; he had seemed so old and stern to her then. And she also remembered his wife, the librarian; a woman with round spectacles and sad eyes, who was often ill.

There was one particular day that Satseko had never forgotten: a winter's afternoon after her mother had taken her tobogganing in the park. Although she'd remembered it often since, she sometimes thought it must have been a dream, as the one time she tried to mention it, Natsuko had immediately silenced her.

It had been almost dusk when they left the park that day, and her mother's teacher was sat in his car outside the gates. It was as though he'd been waiting for them. They drove home along the coast road, hypnotised by the swirling white flakes against the windscreen. She remembered them whispering urgently to each other, the radio drowning out their words. One of her mother's favourite songs started playing, and he looked at her and smiled, before turning up the volume. He stopped the car at the edge of a group of trees, and walked round to Natsuko's door, holding out his hand. Their boots crunched through the snow as they walked to the front of the car; spot-lit in the headlamps. Satseko sat in the back seat, transfixed, watching the snow fall like confetti on her mother's hair, white against the gleaming black. Their footprints formed patterns as they danced back and forth across the beam of the headlights. As the song ended her mother laid her head against Akira's shoulder for a moment, and Satseko broke the spell by getting out of the car and running over to join them. They threw their heads back to catch the snowflakes on their tongues, and Natsuko and Akira had laughed and held out their arms. They all linked hands and formed a circle, and as the next song started they were spinning, spinning, spinning...

Satseko hung the other photograph back on the wall, then took out her phone to call the hospital. While she waited to be connected to the cardiac unit she caught a glimpse of herself in the hallway mirror.

'Hello, Miss Satseko Ito? Sorry to have kept you waiting. Are you the next of kin?'

She continued to look at herself in the mirror. She could see it now.

TO BE THE BEACH

They turned down the narrow road towards the coast and, for a few heedless moments, Lydia almost believed that this break would do them good. That Dean really meant what he said this time. Instinctively she looked down at the raw bruises on her wrists, then touched the raised scar on her neck. Dean reached across and stroked her hand, switching on his familiar lazy smile.

They pulled over for a minute so that he could read the final directions. As they went through the gate that led to the cart track, clouds scudded in from the sea and the afternoon turned dark and cold. They reached a row of bleak caravans, grey-curtained and dirty, crouching low between grass-covered dunes.

The caravan they stopped at was the dirtiest of them all; dented and rusty, with junk piled up behind it. A dead rabbit lay outside the door, bloated and stiff, staring up at the sky through a single cloudy eye. Lydia walked to the edge of the low cliff and looked down at the beach. Stunted trees, misshapen by the wind, clung tenaciously to the cliffs. The sand was littered with thick ropes of seaweed, broken shells, and the curled legs of dead starfish that had been caught out by the tide.

She went inside the caravan. It was damp and dimly lit,

coated with the sour, salty skin of the seaside.

Dean switched on the portable television and slouched in the corner, half-watching the ghostly, fizzing pictures as he flicked through the channels. He opened his first beer, and lined up three more at his side, smiling at her as she busied herself unpacking their groceries.

'Everything'll be ok, Lydia,' he muttered.

She nodded and smiled, exactly as she always did. Then she reached for a saucepan. As she heated up the casserole they had brought, the windows steamed up, and the dusty twilight faded to black behind the fogged glass. Later, when she carried the rubbish outside, she paused to watch the tiny pinpricks of light out at sea. Fishing boats winked on the invisible horizon, the only sign that there was any other life out there. They were too far away to save her.

When Lydia cleaned her teeth, the mottled mirror distorted her face. She was a pale stranger, eyes ringed with black; a ghost in the glass, waiting to be asked in or set free. She wiped the condensation away, looked at the remains of the latest bruises on the side of her neck, and traced the old scar with her finger.

Dean called out to her, his voice slurred by the beer.

'What are you doing in there, Lyd?'

Long after he had rolled over, she lay awake, her face pressed against the stale, yellowed pillow. The trees creaked in the wind; tethered souls, their tangled roots straining to break free.

When she finally fell asleep her dreams were dark and jumbled. She stood on the roof of a dustcart, its sides streaked with thick, brown grease. The crushing mechanism was turning, and she walked towards the end as though she were planning to throw herself in. For a moment she felt relieved; one more step and she would be free. She peered over the edge, with her arms swung forward as though preparing to dive. The wagon was full of dead rabbits. Their fur was matted and congealed with thick, black blood, and each one stared up at her with glowing red eyes. She lurched back, screaming, and woke with a start, her hair stuck to her cheek with sweat. Dean turned and muttered in his sleep, then rolled over. She held her breath until she was sure she hadn't woken him.

Just a few hours later she was forced awake again by the light at sunrise. Dean was snoring heavily into the wall. She crept quietly out of the bedroom and took her jacket from the chair.

It was a perfect morning. The clouds had cleared and the wind had dropped. As she stepped down to the beach she passed a row of upturned rowboats, freshly painted in yellows and reds. She saw flowers still asleep in the grass: daisies, their undersides washed with pink, and the tightly closed petals of waxy celandines.

The sea whispered to her as it lapped and ebbed. The smooth, pale sand was marbled with veins of crushed mussel shells, and freckled with handfuls of small flat stones.

Lydia wanted to be the beach. Every day the sand had her wrinkles smoothed by the sea, her slate wiped clean, her rubbish swept away. She presented herself anew each morning, as though nothing had ever happened there before. As though no dog had ever raced headlong after a ball, leaving untidy paw prints in a skittering arc. As though lovers had never walked hand in hand at the water's edge and stooped to pick up shells.

A lone gull wheeled overhead, sunlight catching the underside of his white wings. The bird's eerie cry mingled with

Dean's voice, shouting to her from the cliff top. She turned with a start, automatically lifting her hand to wave. As she looked up she saw a red helium balloon. It jerked and dived and soared, pulling free, higher and higher, carrying a hand-written message to the world on its fluttering label. Perhaps a child was watching its steady climb from farther along the cliff top, waiting for the moment it disappeared into the blue: hope swallowed whole.

Dean looked down and called her name again. His face was contorted. But she couldn't hear him anymore, she could only see his lips move, and his mouth was black and twisted. For a moment she allowed herself to imagine him slipping off the cliff edge and dashing his head against the jutting rocks.

Farther along the beach a dog was barking, and Lydia turned towards the sound. A collie raced in circles, waiting for his owner to throw a ball, and at the water's edge a young girl combed the seaweed for shells and sea glass. Her sweater was a splash of scarlet against the pale dunes. She was Lydia's own bright, beckoning speck of hope.

She set off slowly, following the girl towards the light-house. At first she looked back, then she picked up speed, leaving a trail of bold footprints along the clean sand. As she neared the harbour she could make out the fish and chip shop, the ice cream parlour, and she could hear laughter above the screech of the gulls. Children raced along the shoreline, and the beach was ribboned with the candy stripes of windbreaks and deckchairs. Lydia sat on the sea wall and watched them, no longer caring whether Dean found her, because she knew she wasn't going back.

JUST ENOUGH LIGHT

Tanya has one arm thrown across the pillow, and her face is turned away from me, hidden beneath a tangle of hair. I step from the cool tiled floor onto the terrace, and watch the fishermen mending their nets on the pier.

At the water's edge the windows of Joe's restaurant are pushed wide open. I imagine the soft sea breeze blowing through the bar and the taste of the fresh lobster. I want to be there now with a cold beer, and I shake Tanya's shoulder.

'Tom?' she whispers, but she doesn't stir.

Downstairs in the kitchen, Maria sweeps the floor, singing to herself. Through the open doorway she can see down the dusty street, and she waves at Joe's wife as she sashays past with her dachshund, his coat as shiny as a newly opened conker.

Maria stops sweeping when she sees me, smiles, and tells me to sit down; she has coffee brewing.

I tell her I have no classes today, and that I want her sister to come out for lunch with me. She shrugs and smiles, then reminds me that the American is coming here to pick up Tanya. That he is taking her to Havana, to the Hotel Nacional, to drink mojitos in the Bar Galeria. That he has promised to take her shopping.

I shake my head and take the coffee pot from the stove. Even in Havana there is nothing to buy. The dresses that Tanya admires in her dog-eared copies of Vogue; no money can buy those here. I want her to sit by the sea with me, to taste the sweet lobster, to talk with the fishermen. She does not want that. She wants to put on her cheap, bright dress and drive up and down the Malecón with the rich American.

It is not enough that I love her. When she sees the plea in my face, her eyes darken and her mouth twists in defiance. But I can't help myself. I couldn't help myself from the start.

There had been a card on the university notice board; Maria was advertising for a foreign student to rent her spare room. On the day I moved in, she sent Tanya to meet me from class to help pick up my things. Tanya wore a red silk flower in her hair, and came with her friend, Elisa, a dancer at the Tropicana who knew someone with a taxi. We walked round to his apartment, and Tanya and I talked while we waited outside for them. She spoke quickly, making no allowances for my limited Spanish. But I didn't miss a word.

I couldn't help myself. Not from the moment we squeezed into the back seat of the car together, wedged in by my rucksack, the warm skin of her shoulder pressing against my arm, or from the moment she turned her head to look out of the window, and I breathed in the scent of her hair.

Later that evening we went down to Joe's, and stayed until late, holding hands across the table. When she looked at me, her eyes shone, and I wound her hair around my fingers and pulled her to me. We drank mojitos and danced on the terrace.

I didn't know about the American, then. Or the others.

But the next day I saw her on the corner talking to the Canadian men who had come down for the fishing contest.

I saw her laugh with them, turn her head to one side, and touch their arms lightly with her fingertips. She disappeared that night until 4 a.m. and wouldn't answer me when I asked where she'd been. Since then she has stayed out late many times, including last night, and I have learned not to ask questions. Occasionally, she bothers to invent a vague explanation, and I just nod in response to each lie.

I pour my coffee and watch Maria as she sweeps the veranda. Tanya walks into the room and fetches a cup, then sits next to me at the table. She is wearing her tight pink dress, and her hair is tied up with a blue ribbon. She doesn't speak.

The kitchen shutters are half-closed and there's just enough light to see Tanya's face when the American pulls up outside. But I don't want to see the look in her eyes. I don't want to see her eagerness to go with him rather than me. I don't want to see that she thinks he is someone special.

He will flatter her and lay his money down, make idle promises to marry her and take her to America. She will let him squeeze her firm thigh with his fat hand as they eat spicy pork in La Guarida, but she will still turn her head each time the door opens, and through the haze of cigar smoke she will watch everyone as they arrive and leave. There is always the chance of an even more promising prize. Tanya's eye is sharp and, like a magpie, she's always searching for the next bright trinket.

Later, she'll let him take her back to his hotel, and then come home to me in the early hours, trying to crawl between the sweat-damp sheets without waking me. In the solid stillness before dawn, I'll feel the heat of her skin against my back and pretend to be asleep, knowing that in the morning, as always, I will only remember I love her and not how I felt the night before.

***

I hide my face in the pillow when I hear Tom stir. He can't see me until I've covered the bruises with make-up. I need to dress alone so he doesn't see the welts on my thighs. He shakes my shoulder but I pretend to be half-asleep, mutter his name and turn away. I can't face going downstairs but the rich American from the Nacional is coming, so I must.

I can feel the ache and pull in my ribcage as I sit up, the sting of my still-swollen lips, and a deeper pain in my core, at the heart of me, that has no physical cause and maybe no cure.

I did my best to please the Canadian, not wanting to annoy him until he had handed over the twenty dollars. I stayed on the bed with him, his flabby pale skin pressed against me, as I waited patiently for him to reach for his wallet.

I picked him up in the Sunset Bar; he was an easy target. Then we went back to Elisa's place. It's too risky for a Cuban to be seen with a foreigner in a tourist hotel. He had followed me at a distance as I asked. I knew he wasn't happy, but he wanted me enough to comply. He looked around as he came into the apartment, took in the worn, sagging couch, the chipped stove and the faded curtains. He walked over to the open window, looking out of place and uncomfortable, too large for the room.

'Where's the bedroom?' he asked.

I led him out onto the balcony instead, fetched Elisa's rum, and suggested we sat for a while with a drink. If they like you, they treat you better. He leant on the rusty railing and looked across the narrow street. An old woman watched us from a doorway, son music drifting from her radio. Down in the alleyway two rake-thin girls were arguing over something and nothing, their high-pitched voices carrying on the night air.

He turned back inside, downing his drink as he went, and pulled me up with his other arm.

'Come on, girl, I ain't got all night.'

I did what I always did. Fixed my face into a seductive smile, switched my mind to elsewhere. I thought about how one day I wouldn't be in Havana. I'd live in America and have everything I wanted: freedom, pretty clothes, and a good Cuban man who would be kind to me.

The man undressed, leaving his clothes where they fell.

'Get over here girl and stop messing around.'

I slid my dress over my head and drew the thin curtains. Then I lay on the bed and waited for him. He grunted and heaved over me, taking his time, leaning in close to kiss me. I turned my head away.

'Extra for kissing,' I said.

'Ok, ok, I'll pay the extra.' He thrust his mouth towards me again.

'Twenty dollars in total,' I said. I needed to be sure.

I have to buy good clothes to please the American. He's my ticket to Miami. And then I'll leave him and find a nice Cuban boy. I'll find Ernesto Angel, who left Havana with his family when I was only seventeen. He's the only boy who's ever cared about me.

Apart from Tom. But though Tom is sweet, he has no money.

When the Canadian finished I waited patiently for his breathing to slow, for him to put on his shorts and shirt and leave the notes on the side.

He heaved himself up on one arm and looked at me.

I waited.

'Twenty dollars, you said?'

I nodded as he reached for his wallet.

'Twenty is more than a cheap girl like you is worth. But I'm feeling generous. I'll give you ten if you kick me out now, twenty if you let me stay and we play to my rules.'

I thought of the candy pink houses in Miami. Every dollar was another step towards freedom, and Ernesto's smile.

After he left I lay quiet. It was as I expected - only a single ten dollar bill pushed under the chipped statuette of Our Lady. Her watchful eyes reproached me so I turned her to face the wall.

My wrists were rubbed raw where he had held me so tightly. My lips were swollen and I could taste blood. But I managed to get up and walk through the dark streets back to the safety of my sister's house, and Tom.

And now I know they are sat in the kitchen, waiting for me while I dress to go out with the American, applying my make-up with extra care.

The shutters are drawn against the sun, and the kitchen is cool and dark. When I sit at the table with my coffee, there is just enough light to see Tom's face, to see the love written bright in his eyes, despite everything.

I imagine sitting at the water's edge, at Joe's bar, and feeling the sea breeze on my bare shoulders. I imagine Tom's fingers intertwined with mine.

I decide that I'll tell the American I can't go anywhere with him today. I'll send Maria out to the car to say I'm ill. Just this one time.

SOMETHING ELSE ENTIRELY

Miranda had read about the Russian chapel in Will's guide book. It was signposted at the crossroads beyond the village, and they had decided to walk there, through the valley and up the steep road that eventually led to the mountain pass.

Miranda liked to hear the clang and jangle of cowbells on the lower slopes, and to see the alpine flowers scattered amongst the tall grass. Where the grass had been cut, it was hanging to dry on wooden hayracks. The farmhands shouted across the fields to them and Miranda waved back. Will said that all the country boys were in love with her, and they both laughed. The sun had bleached her hair the colour of corn, and she let it hang loose, the way he liked it. He called her his pale angel.

When they reached the steep path they passed two farmers carrying heavy hay rakes; both of the men were tall, lithe and dark-eyed. Shirts tied around their waists revealed muscled shoulders turned honey-gold in the sun. They nodded to Miranda and after they passed by she could hear their laughter echoing across the hillside. She told Will that she thought them rude, but he just smiled and kissed her forehead.

She hung back, gazing down the road after the farmers,

thinking about all the men that she would never meet, and those that she would meet, but would have to turn away.

She thought of Aldo, their neighbour at the villa outside Venice. He had stood at the fence offering basil and tomatoes when they arrived, his dark eyes appraising Miranda as they talked. He bowed to her, kissed her hand, and she found herself blushing. He had asked them to his brother's restaurant that same evening and Miranda had drunk too much wine and flirted openly. She had untied her hair and let it fall against Aldo's arm as he rested it along her chair back, imagining the taste of his lips and the feel of his rough workman's hands.

As she thought of the Italian, she watched Will striding away from her up the steep path towards the chapel and smiled to herself. She was lucky. He was patient with her, and made her feel safe. Sometimes, at night, when they lay together in the half-dark, he looked towards the sky as though in prayer, and his fear of losing her slept silently at their side. She knew that it should be enough.

They crossed a narrow bridge spanning a fast alpine stream. White water tumbled down the vertical rock. Miranda crouched at its side and felt the sharp cold race through her fingers. She was happy to be in the mountains after the narrow alleyways of Venice, although at least in Italy there had been just the two of them, itself a relief to her after the cosmopolitan chatter of the café life in Nice. Will had known many of the other guests at the Hotel Renee, and every night they had strolled along the Promenade des Anglais together and finished their evenings with brandy and coffee in the Cafe Jardin. The women's laughter was shrill and their conversation pointless. She disliked the way they put a hand on their husband's arm if they wanted something. The men would glance down absentmindedly at their long red nails and nod in agreement to whatever they'd asked.

Miranda had been invisible to these women. They looked through her as though she were a ghost, trying to deny the existence of anyone prettier and younger than themselves.

Will shouted down to her now, interrupting her thoughts. He said he could see the chapel ahead, above the road. She ran to catch him up.

They climbed the steps and stopped, silent, by the tomb. Then they went inside the tiny wooden church where Miranda lit a candle. She told him that it was for the souls of all the Russian prisoners of war that had died there in an avalanche in 1916.

He took the guide book and sat on the wall outside. Miranda stayed behind and, although she was not religious, she stood in silent prayer in front of the faded icons on the altar. She prayed for her husband, for their marriage, and for herself. She knew that Will had pinned his hopes on her; on his angel. In her prayers she promised to be different this time, asked for the strength she needed to keep that promise.

**

That evening they went down to the hotel bar. They talked quietly in the corner, holding hands, hardly glancing up at the other guests as they came in or went out. The American couple at the bar remarked to one another how much in love the honeymooners seemed to be, and that it was delightful to see, although they were surprised at how much older he was than her. Miranda stood up to fetch two more drinks. She swayed a little, the beer had gone straight to her head as it always did. She laughed as she steadied herself against the wall, then leant over to kiss Will. He pushed her away, aware that people were staring. He said they should go to their room, but she wouldn't leave with him. She walked over to the bar and ordered another beer.

'I want to go dancing,' she said, twisting her arms above her head and clicking her fingers to an imagined rhythm.

Will noticed two men at the next table watching them, so he stood and held out his hand to her. She took it and tried to push him back down. He stumbled against the table and sent his empty beer bottle crashing to the floor. She laughed at him and still refused to leave. He walked away and said that he would see her back at the room.

After he left, the two men came over with another beer for her and sat down. They were the farmers she'd seen that morning on the road. They smiled and nodded to her, but only understood a few words of English. She told the barman to ask them to take her dancing, and then rested her head on the shoulder of the younger man.

The barman told her that they knew of a place she could dance, at a hotel at the other end of the village. She jumped up and clapped her hands, pulling them to their feet and taking each one by the arm.

The men talked to each other quietly as they walked through the village, and Miranda stayed silent. Inside the hotel, one of them led her to the dance floor while the other went for drinks. There was a slow song playing and he pulled her tightly against him, breathing heavily into her hair. She clung to him and they stood there together, swaying to the music.

Afterwards, she let him lead her outside into the field and lay her down in the grass. Under the black sky, his eyes were ovals of polished jet, and she shivered. He was not as gentle as her new husband, and he pinned her arms above her head, clasping each of her hands in his own. She remembered the inside of the chapel, and imagined the candles snuffed out by her broken promise, and the faded Madonna disappearing into the darkness. But as she wrapped her thighs around this stranger, she didn't care; he made her feel alive, and sometimes Will appeared so distant, across a space too wide to cross.

She lay beside the farmer, inhaling the musty scent of cut hay. Before he dressed, she knelt over him, her palms pressed together; a fallen angel in the moonlight.

When Miranda got back to the hotel room, Will was waiting up for her. She decided to tell him about the farmers and the dancing, and hoped he'd understand. It was better to tell him now, in case someone from the hotel mentioned they had seen her. The American couple had watched her leave, and there were probably others.

But Will was in no mood to let it go. He had been back down to the bar to look for her, had already been told where she'd gone. He had felt everyone's eyes on him, had known they were all laughing behind his back. Laughing at the middle-aged man who couldn't control his young wife. He paced the room, his jealousy thumping through the floor, and they argued until they fell asleep, exhausted.

***

When they woke, the sun was already bright. Miranda turned towards Will, but he lay with his back to her, all hope drained from him, and as soon as she touched him he swung his legs out of bed and went to the bathroom.

They had already organised the hire of a taxi for the day to take them down to Lake Bled. When Miranda suggested they should cancel the plan, Will met her gaze with red-rimmed eyes and insisted that they should still go.

They ate their breakfast in silence and didn't make eye contact. Will got up to fetch more coffee without asking Miranda if she wanted a cup. The restaurant was busy, and she was conscious of their awkwardness, but when she glanced round no one appeared to have noticed them.

In reality, they were being closely observed by the American couple.

'Tramp,' muttered the woman.

Her husband smiled. 'I prefer to think of her as a free spirit,' he said.

She cradled her coffee cup in both hands and peered at him over the rim. 'Well, whatever you think, I see an unhappy ending there. I feel sorry for that man.'

***

After breakfast, Miranda waited on the seat outside the hotel entrance while Will went back for his guidebook. The sun was warm on her face and she could smell the overpowering scent of the flowers in the garden. The day was coming alive.

She watched the American walk arm in arm with his wife, guiding her towards a taxi where her friend was waiting. He waved at them as the car pulled away, and strolled back towards the door, stopping in front of her.

'My wife's gone sightseeing to Ljubljana. That's me at a loose end for the day. What about you, angel?'

Miranda met his gaze; the cool, steady gaze of this man who called her angel, but whose voice suggested he thought her something else entirely. In his eyes she saw Aldo and the Slovenian farmers, and the baker in Tuscany who had waited every evening in his doorway for her, hoping that she would come to him. She saw every man that she had ever wanted or refused, and every man to whom she had ever said yes.

When Will came out and indicated the waiting taxi, she stood up, but then paused. The American was still watching her as he walked back into the lobby. Will looked round, and his expression switched from impatience to fear. He knew she wasn't coming.

'I can't do this today, Will. I think it's better if we each have some time on our own. You go without me. I'm sorry.'

She went back inside before he could answer, watched through the glass doors until she saw the taxi draw away.

'It seems that I'm at a loose end too,' she said to the American.

PINK KNICKERS

I saw you today. I passed by the barber shop in town, and there you were, sat in a chair by the window. You looked exactly as I remembered, only ten years older; your broad nose still freckled, and that same easy grin as you chatted to the girl cutting your hair. Shamelessly flirting; talking to her reflection with your hands and your eyes. I paused at the window for a moment, hoping you'd look up.

Then reality kicked in; there was no way that it could have been you. And even if there had been that possibility, it's over forty years since I last saw you. You'd be fifty-four now, not twenty-four.

The last time I saw you I was thirteen and you were fourteen. I wasn't allowed to hang out with you. You were on my mother's 'That' list, right up there in the top ten. You were 'That Ian Armstrong,' tempting and forbidden.

I wasn't allowed to go into the disused quarry either, but one afternoon in the summer holidays I found myself stuck halfway up the cliff face, my plimsolls mired in heavy clay. The yellow-grey mud underneath my fingernails and in my hair, smeared across my jeans and jacket.

And I was frightened. You were shouting from above, encouraging and threatening in equal measure.

I couldn't let you see I was scared. But there was no way

up and no way down. I clung hopelessly to a thin branch of broom and felt the tears well up as the thorns bit into my palms.

Then you were stretching down, reaching out for me with your sticky grey hand. I held it tightly and hauled myself up those last few feet to the top. With a final pull, you saw me safely over the overhang, and then abruptly let go and flung yourself down onto the thick couch grass.

I had never been up there before. I could see into the back gardens of the council houses that ran along the edge of the field beyond the quarry, and up on the top were a row of sheds and neatly marked out allotments.

You jumped up.

'Come on,' you said, 'let's go and see what we can find.'

You walked over to the first shed and peered through the window with your hand cupped against the glass. There was no one around but the allotments were all well-tended. This one had rows of peas, pale green lettuces and thick-skinned broad beans. Honeysuckle climbed a trellis on the fence.

You tried the door to the shed, which was held by a small padlock. You pulled it half-heartedly, shrugged. 'Nothing much in there anyway,' you said.

I admit I was relieved. I didn't want you to take anything.

At the end of the row of allotments there was a stack of stuff piled into a makeshift bonfire, next to a large compost heap. On the bonfire there was an old washstand. Its marble top had been hacked off and left at the side but there were still tiles on the wooden splash-back, decorated with lush red peonies and deep orange marigolds. I ran my fingers over the raised pattern.

You looked over my shoulder.

'Do you want one?' you asked.

I nodded.

'What's it worth?'

I could feel my heart thudding. This was why my mother told me not to speak to you or any of your friends. She always said you would want me to do things I didn't want to do; things that I mustn't let you do.

But I wanted the tile.

'I'll let you kiss me,' I said, feeling my cheeks flush. I looked at your mouth as I said it, wondering how it would taste on mine. I imagined your hot mid-afternoon breath tasting of dunked biscuits, malty and sweet.

I was a late starter. I'd only kissed a boy once; Kevin Pearson, behind the dusty velvet curtains at the school dance. Do you remember him? He had a pasty complexion and home-knitted gloves fastened to his duffle coat pockets with plaited wool.

But in the giddy excitement of my first dance he seemed attractive in his new blue shirt and Levi's. His hand was warm in mine as he led me over to the long curtains by the window. And behind those curtains, with my back pressed awkwardly against the sharp metal window frame, we kissed all night. They were kisses for kissing's sake. They weren't meant to arouse passion or express love. They were exploratory kisses. Ones that were meant for tasting, for rolling around the mouth and savouring. They were kisses that simply led to more kisses. Kisses that made my mouth sore, kisses that made my tongue swell. Beautiful teenage kisses.

But when I said you could kiss me, you looked at me oddly.

You got out your small penknife and slid the blade down between the top tile and the cracked wood backing. I saw it give slightly, and you flexed the knife. Then you stopped and looked at me again, squinting against the sun.

'Let me put my hand in your knickers,' you said.

It was a statement, not a question. That was the payment for the tile. I didn't feel I had a choice, but I didn't want one. It was exciting to be up there with you, watching the sunlight dance on your soft brown hair.

'Ok,' I whispered.

You took my hand and led me round the back of the shed where the honeysuckle was growing. There was a single sun-flower in a pot, its head hanging heavy with the fullness and weight of its seeds.

'Lie down over there,' you said.

I shook my head.

'Tile first.'

'Wait here then.'

I could have run, I could have changed my mind, and I know you would have just shrugged and smiled. But I waited for you to come back, inhaling the heady scent of the honey-suckle, telling myself that it would be alright.

You returned with two tiles. They were beautiful. Deep, deep green, gold and crimson. Crackled, crazed glaze. You threw them down on the grass next to me.

'Lie down then,' you said.

I lay down without a word.

You flopped down next to me and wiped the clay off your hands as best you could, without me having to ask. Then you leant over and kissed me. It was a clumsy kiss, your teeth grating against mine, your tongue trying to find a way inside my mouth. You tasted of summer and earth.

When I felt your hand on my stomach, I jumped. You left it there a moment until I lay still and I decided to let you do whatever you wanted.

You unfastened my jeans and pushed your hand inside my knickers. I felt your fingers dancing across my skin, almost tickling, and I held my breath until you took your hand out. You muttered something that sounded like 'thanks'.

I was disappointed. I thought I would feel different in some way, yet I was still Sandra, laid in the grass with my pink cotton knickers on show.

But I had something good to tell Julie and Susan. I had gone further with a boy than they had, and I knew Susan would be jealous.

And I had the tiles, the beautiful tiles with the art deco flowers. But I didn't know where I would tell my mother I had got them from, or how I'd explain the clay on my new pink knickers.

I wanted to keep you up there a while longer, so I reached into my jacket pocket for the Rizla tin with the rolling machine in the lid. The one that I had stolen from my dad's drawer the last time I was there. Julie had brought round some of her grandad's tobacco, and we had practiced rolling cigarettes in my bedroom.

I passed the tin to you, but you pushed it back across the grass to me.

'Roll one for me will you?' you said.

You lay back down, crossing your arms behind your head and closing your eyes against the sun. Even though you weren't watching, my hand shook as I took a liquorice paper from the packet and a finger of tobacco from the tin.

You held the finished cigarette up and examined it with a grin.

'Not bad.'

You smoked it as though it was a special cigar, holding it out and examining it between drags. I loved you for that.

That was the moment I knew.

Then you reached for my hand to pull me up, and I felt a shiver run through me.

'Can we come up here again?' I asked.

You smiled. That bemused, lop-sided smile.

'Yes, Sandra Broadbent,' you said, 'we can come up here again.'

You started to clamber down the cliff ahead of me, and I stumbled after you, trying to hide my daft grin. But you rushed ahead, slipping and sliding down the clay bank without looking back.

I started to slide down behind you, clutching the tiles and reaching out for a tuft of couch grass with my free hand. I wanted to call out and ask you to help me, but it came out as a squeak, and you were disappearing below the ridge.

I couldn't stop myself from falling any longer, and as the thick slick of greasy clay fell away beneath me, I screamed. You turned to look at me just as I dropped one of the tiles. It went flying over the edge of the ridge. As you ducked to avoid it I saw your forehead smash into a jutting tree stump. Blood spurted bright against your pale skin, then you lay still.

I slid past you and came to a stop in the blackberry bushes at the bottom. I lay there for a minute. My leg hurt and the thorns were jabbing into my arm. The remaining tile lay at the side of me, cracked, but still in one piece.

I was shaking, every breath a gasp, every heartbeat hammering against bone. But I knew I couldn't stay there. Nobody would find us if I didn't get help. I stood, testing my leg. I had twisted it, but I instinctively knew that it wasn't broken. I also knew that you were badly hurt and that, consequently, I was in serious trouble.

In the telephone box at the end of the road I turned the

dial round to 9. Then I paused as I caught sight of my reflection in the glass. My arms and legs were smeared with thick yellow clay. I'd messed with the big boys and I was about to be caught out. I would be in the worst trouble of my life. I let go of the dial abruptly, and started to replace the receiver.

But as I was about to put it down I snatched it back. I couldn't leave you there. I turned the dial round twice more to 9, and whispered directions to the operator as to where to send an ambulance. I wouldn't tell them my name. Then I ran home, getting there just minutes before my mother was due back from work. I hid my clothes under the bed, took fresh jeans from the drawer and quickly ran a bath. As I climbed into the water I heard the ambulance race by on its way to the hospital.

It was only much later that evening that I remembered the tile. I had left it in the phone box, on the shelf with the directories.

I went back the next day, but it had gone. So I walked around the bottom of the quarry to see if I could find the other tile; the one that had slipped from my hand. It was there, miraculously unbroken. I carried it home and hid it under the bed with my dirty clothes.

When the local paper asked for the girl who had called the ambulance to come forward, my mother didn't say a word. And her silence told me that she knew.

Two weeks later I took the tile to the cemetery, wrapped in my pink knickers, and laid it down beside the wilting flowers on the raw mound of your grave.

NO LONGER CHARLOTTE

The unclaimed rucksack continued its endless loop around the baggage carousel. Every time it reappeared through the strip curtains it offered a moment of hope for Charlotte. She took a half step forward in anticipation, and then slumped back again when she realised it wasn't her case. The airport was hot and dusty, a trickle of sweat snaked down her back, and she was impatient to be outside in the Italian sunshine. Eventually, a passing porter swung the rucksack to the ground and carried it to the far desk. With nothing left to offer, the conveyor juddered to a halt. Hope stopped with it.

Charlotte followed the porter to the counter, pulling the docket from the back of her passport to present to the clerk, who told her the case would be delivered to Villa Il Bordini as soon as they located it. She sounded confident that it would be found immediately. Subito!

Charlotte looked down at her crumpled shirt and jeans. This was not the outfit she wanted to wear for her dinner reservation that night. Yet she didn't have enough spare cash for another new dress. Her mother, Isabella, had booked and paid for this Italian trip several months ago - 'To cheer you up, darling, after I'm gone' - and when she died just three weeks later, Charlotte discovered that she'd spent almost every penny she had. Isabella had wanted to keep up appearances, to be the best version of herself she could possibly manage right until the end. No one would have denied her that, yet Charlotte couldn't help wondering if any of it really mattered. It was the things hidden from sight that were important, the things you saw with your heart.

So what would Isabella do right now? Her mother would lie, of course.

She called the insurance company from the taxi, saying she had a vital business appointment first thing in the morning and needed appropriate clothes. Thanks to her mother's generous insurance policy a significant amount of money was transferred to her account straight away.

Villa Il Bordoni was beautiful in every way Isabella had been and that Charlotte wasn't. It was understated with remarkable bone structure. The pale, polished marble floors, the peonies in cut glass vases, the glimpses of lush green gardens between the stone pillars of the colonnade.

In the lobby Charlotte noticed a young woman wearing an elegant shift dress. Red linen, patterned with perfect polka dots: not so small as to be little more than apologetic punctuation, yet not so large as to be clownish. Perfectly cut at the neck, falling straight over slender hips. The woman had white blonde hair in an elfin cut. She was androgynous, a girl-boy-boy-girl, and she commanded the attention of everyone in the room. She seemed unaware of their scrutiny, and if she was aware of it then nothing about her betrayed that knowledge. There was no vanity or arrogance in her stance, she was simply someone at ease in their skin. And as Isabella had often remarked, there is nothing more beautiful than a confident woman.

Charlotte thought of her safe floral tea dress in the lost

suitcase. She would never find anything like that here. Isabella would be teasing her now; impatient with her daughter's unease, her gaucheness, encouraging her to try something a little braver.

She went to the bar and ordered a gin and tonic, and afterwards she headed out into town. She smiled at the concierge, but he didn't give her a second glance. The late afternoon sun slanted through the gaps between the shuttered buildings, seeking out the hidden piazzas, and dancing across the glittering fountains. She saw the shops that sold almost nothing, the ones where you had to pluck up courage to ring the doorbell. But there was nowhere that someone like Charlotte could buy a dress.

A church bell chimed, and there was a flutter of white wings above her head. She glanced up, and noticed the painting of the Madonna on the wall of the building at the corner of the street. It was high up, out of reach, even if you leant out from the upper windows, yet mysteriously there was a votive candle burning in a glass holder beneath it. Then she saw the dress. Dark cobalt blue, patterned with exactly the right size polka dots, displayed on a dressmaker's dummy in the second floor window, and a sign on the street door pointed up to Maria's, a tiny atelier reached by a narrow flight of steps. As she entered the room, the faint tinkle of a bell could be heard above the door, and after a moment a woman appeared in an apron covered with pins. In her hands she held a pair of soft suede pumps in forest green.

'They are perfect!' Charlotte said, and the seamstress laughed.

When she took the dress from the window, Charlotte saw that the circles were not polka dots at all, but the tiniest embroidered flowers. She tried it on behind a velvet curtain, and stepped out to look in the mirror. It skimmed her curves and showed off the gentle dips above her collar bones. She appeared taller, improbably chic; still Charlotte, yet a different version. In that moment everything was sharply focussed, colours more vivid, and she suddenly understood that the future could be brighter too. She turned round, grinning, and Maria clapped her hands. Molto bella! She held the dress in a little at the back and smiled at Charlotte's reflection, waiting for approval. Charlotte nodded. By the time she had changed back into her jeans the dress was already being altered, and in moments there were two small darts added.

The green shoes were a size too small, but Maria found her another pair - handmade by her brother, she said - and these were the deepest red. A petite red suede clutch bag that matched them, Maria told her was regalo-omaggio - a free gift.

Next door there was a hairdresser. No appointment necessary. She asked the woman to cut her hair molto corto. Very short. Like a boy's. And to dye it white blonde. Bionda bianca.

As her hair fell to the floor around her, she felt herself become someone else. Without Isabella to see her, to outshine her, she could finally become whoever she wanted to be. She was no longer Charlotte.

When she stepped back outside she looked up as she crossed the street, blowing a kiss to the Madonna and the curious candle that had guided her to Maria's shop.

When she arrived back at the hotel she was suddenly impatient, and she changed in a hurry, leaving her clothes strewn on the floor as she slipped into the dress. She stepped into the red shoes, and tucked her money and her lipstick inside the clutch bag. Then she smiled at herself in the mirror and ran her fingers through her new hair.

Now she understood why appearances were important to her mother. It wasn't the clothes themselves that attracted attention, it was the way they made her feel and act that impelled people to respond to her the way they did. Isabella had always shone.

Charlotte went to the desk to cancel her dinner reservation on the way out, and the concierge rushed over to help her. She was suddenly visible, and yet Il Bordini was now too elegant, too restrained, for her new persona. She wanted to be back out on the streets in the velvet dusk, amongst the chatter and throng, the clack of heels on the smooth, worn cobbles, the chink of glasses, the drift of perfume, scarlet-lipped smiles, and the scent of mimosa. She wanted to test out her new self in the remnants of this day; the warm afternoon drifting seamlessly into evening, offering the promise of something wonderful, magical, behind every doorway, and through every archway. In the side streets, doors opened and closed, and friends and lovers stepped out into the street, already drunk with the scent and thrum of the evening. Their voices and their laughter echoed around the narrow streets, and they reached for each other's hands.

Charlotte had asked the concierge to recommend a restaurant for an early supper, and she followed his scribbled map to a square by the canal. Even though it was early, half a dozen people were waiting for tables at the bar. They asked if she had a reservation, but even when she said no they led her straight through to the main room, moved chairs aside, and swung a small table across into a corner. Heads turned, tracking her progress as she crossed the floor to her seat.

She ate fish cooked with olives and almonds, drank half

a carafe of house white, and felt invincible. She loved the attention of the waiters, the unguarded stares from men and women alike. She loved being alone in this crowd, and her newfound self-containment.

Back out in the street she found herself caught up in a group of Scandinavians who asked her to go for a drink with them, and she went without a thought. They crossed over a high-arched wooden bridge strung with fairy lights. Tables lined the edge of the canal, but the group headed inside to the bar. Charlotte perched on a stool, cross-legged, and watched herself in the mirror beyond the counter. She turned her head left and right, saw the way her haircut sharpened her chin and slimmed her face, and brought out a vibrancy, a vivacity, that she hadn't known was there. The Scandinavians spoke English for her, and Erik asked her back to their villa, where the beds were still unmade, the table strewn with empty glasses, and the garden filled with the heavy scent of Italian cypress. And she didn't care about the time or the drunkenness, only about the line of fine blond hairs that ran down the centre of Erik's chest, the curve of his neck, and the weight of him on her. And when Sigrid climbed into the bed with them she was suddenly a boy, or perhaps a girl, but never herself; never Charlotte.

And the next day she walked back to Il Bordini, stopping for pastries and coffee on the way. She loved that the waiters served her straight away, that they met her eye, and that when they smiled, they smiled for something other than just their tip. Men looked up from their newspapers and didn't look back down again. Men with impossibly white shirt cuffs, and impossibly sharp suits, men with beautiful grey hair and the darkest eyelashes.

As she passed the atelier she glanced up at the Madonna

one last time. It was then that she noticed the thin wire that ran around the corner of the building. The candle was in fact a flickering bulb. She shrugged her shoulders and smiled. It hadn't been magical after all, but it hardly mattered now.

When she asked for her key at reception, they told her that her suitcase had been delivered to her room. Yet when she opened it, she felt nothing for her things; for the blouses and the tea dress and the sensible sandals, for the rose cologne and the mother of pearl earrings that had pinned her to a sensible life. And when she checked out, she left the clothes in a pile on the unmade bed, and took her case home almost empty.

She knew it wasn't true that she was no longer Charlotte. She'd actually become her definitive self, and she could be that woman with or without the blue dress. She had stepped out from Isabella's shadow to become her best self. And she knew that her mother would approve.

When she opened the case again in the grey light of her London flat, it filled the room with the gold light of Italy, and the faintest trace of Sigrid's lemon cologne. It filled the room with hope.

THE NEXT AND FINAL STOP

The branch line to Onokatsu followed the route of the winding river, and the carriages tilted around tight bends that suddenly tipped the train into mountain tunnels. Occasionally Yume caught glimpses of graceful cranes, their black-tipped wings lit by the sun.

At each station there was a new collection and deposit of chattering schoolchildren, part-time office workers heading home from the bigger towns, and grandmothers weighed down with bags of daikon and cabbage.

Until now, Yume had seldom left the city for more than a week, and she was full of curiosity and apprehension in equal measure. Her best friend, Suki, who had married just three months earlier, had promised to visit, but they were both wise enough to know that their new lives would make this difficult.

When she left for her honeymoon, Yume's father had only nodded and kissed her briefly on the cheek. He couldn't look her in the eye. Her mother had cried and handed her two jars filled with her homemade bean jam. Yume had been embarrassed when her new husband, Otome, had found them in her suitcase. Her mother had never been good at making anko, it was always too dark in colour, and had a strange aftertaste. Otome laughed, said she would never need jam in

Onokatsu as the women in his family made enough to feed the whole of Shikoku island.

Her mother had also insisted on a trousseau of several kimono, sure that her daughter would need them in such a backwater village, where old customs and traditions would still be part of everyday life. Yume had laughed, but secretly she looked forward to wearing the beautifully embroidered pink silk houmongi and the pale green komon scattered with butterflies.

Otome put his hand over hers, and she shivered at the cool touch of his fingers. She turned to the window and watched her new world scroll by: a narrow vine bridge spanning the river below, its rough-hewn planks separated by gaps as wide as giants' feet, paddy fields glinting like emeralds, trees weighed heavy with oranges, and rice straw drying on splay-legged racks, creating the illusion of huge shaggy beasts.

He stroked the back of her hand with the tip of his finger, just as he had done at breakfast on the morning after their wedding night. For a moment, Yume felt her guilt return. When their marriage was arranged her father told Otome and his parents that she'd had no experience of men.

Her father was a businessman from a traditional Osaka family, and there were expectations that his two daughters would marry within the circle of friends and acquaintances that formed his social and business network. But the man her father had lined up for her, Otome Kushida, was much older than her, and Yume wanted to continue her career as an English translator. She had seen how bored her elder sister was with her life in suburbia, and she had rebelled, forming a relationship with Hitoshi, an anime filmmaker. Her mother had met him, and admitted to liking him, but had warned Yume never to let her father hear of him, and not to fall in love.

And although Yume was in love with the idea of Hitoshi, something held her back. He was like free-form jazz, his mind racing off at tangents. He had no attention span or melody she could follow, and was only interested in his own ideas. She yearned for someone to pay her attention, to treat her with respect. Otome Kushida was a man who would do that; a man akin to her own father. Yet she knew it would be too easy to bow to pressure, and for several weeks she delayed her decision.

One afternoon, as they lay in Hitoshi's bed, his mind elsewhere and already making plans for the next day, she tossed a coin.

Her father was delighted with the result, and her marriage to Otome was arranged without anyone ever knowing about her previous lover.

They had honeymooned for four days at the grandest hot spring resort in the Iya Valley. Their room jutted out over the mountainside, and the floor-to-ceiling windows had panoramic views across the valleys and peaks that changed colour in the morning and evening light. Otome had been attentive and gentle, mistaking Yume's quiet demeanour for fear. On their wedding night he had asked for dinner to be served in the room, and as soon as the last dishes were cleared he had led her to the private bath tub on the veranda. Afterwards, they lay down by the window, Yume's silk robe spread beneath her on the tatami matting as the sun slipped silently behind the mountains. It was different to her experience with the filmmaker, and as they lay together in the fading light she believed she could be happy. Hitoshi had never been truly there in the moment. He was always distracted, thinking about his next idea, jumping out of bed to scribble a sketch or write something in his notebook. Otome made her feel that she was all that mattered.

The train slowed down again, and the guard announced the next and final stop as Onokatsu. Otome gathered their cases together and stood by the door. Yume was suddenly nervous. Today she would meet her husband's parents again and see the traditional wooden house where she was to live, the house where she was expected to bring up their children.

Rain pattered down on the deserted station. In the fore-court four battered palm trees bowed towards the sea. Yume couldn't tell whether their cracked brown leaves were whispering a welcome or a warning. There was a lone taxi waiting and when the driver saw them he stepped out to help with their luggage. As the car doors closed, the world was hushed, and Yume was suspended in limbo between her old life and what lay ahead.

Almost immediately, their taxi stopped at traffic lights, and a young mother crossed the road in front of them, guiding a pram with one hand as she huddled beneath her umbrella, her legs splashed with rain. As she reached the other side, she turned, and the two women's eyes met. For a moment Yume could see the bones of this woman's life: a skeleton formed of disappointments and hopes, compromises and longing. She realised that her hand had closed over the door handle, and she snatched it away and placed it back in her lap.

Otome pressed both his hands over hers, and she looked up at him. It was too soon to tell whether he would protect her or possess her, too soon to guess if he would spend his evenings drinking in hostess bars, or whether he would let her be her own person while standing by her side.

As the lights changed and the taxi pulled away, Yume twisted round and waved through the rear window. The woman smiled and lifted her hand in return.

IN THE DARKNESS

Amy shook her umbrella at the door, then fought her way along the bar to the back of the room. Half a dozen men sat at the counter, already filling the tiny space with their clutter of raincoats and briefcases, the musky scent of their day-old sweat, and the buzz of their beer-talk. This early evening sound was always a bright, high thrum - an upbeat rhythm of expectant anticipation. Then came the low notes with the long exhale; the collective sigh of relief at the end of another long, bleached-out day.

She sat down at the end of the counter, on her usual stool under the slope of the staircase. Nori nodded to her and took a tumbler from the shelf. He held up the glass and waited for confirmation before setting up her first whisky, then placed a bowl of rice crackers in front of her, and a fresh, cold towel.

Amy cooled her wrists with the towel, then ran her finger down the outside of the whisky glass, tracing patterns in the condensation, anticipating the fire of the spirit and the snap and pop of the ice.

Each evening she watched the groups of salarymen come and go: dark suits, black shoes, white shirts. They unfastened the top buttons of their shirts as they took their seats, yanked their ties undone as they lifted their glasses, shouted kanpai, and downed their first cold beer. Nori would fetch bowls of ramen from the kitchen, and after they'd eaten they would order a whisky. Then another. Eventually they would

117

stagger out into the night and a new group would tumble in. Amy watched them all, but she was only looking for one.

His name was Koji, and he worked in a department store down the road from the bar. She had been there to buy writing paper one afternoon and he had opened the cabinets to show her the exquisite handmade notebooks, the ink stones, and the lacquered pens. He lifted each item gently from the display case and presented it to her with both hands; offering everything up like a series of precious gifts. There was a tautness to him, a precision in everything he did, underlined by a supple grace. He carried himself like a dancer.

When he handed Amy the receipt for her paper, she read his name at the bottom of the slip.

'Thank you, Koji. Arigato gozaimasu.'

She went into the store again the following week to buy pens and a leather notebook. When she left she handed him a card for Nori's bar that she had slipped into her purse the night before. She didn't hold it out with both hands as etiquette demanded but slid it across to him on the polished desk and, as he picked it up, their fingertips touched.

'Do you know it?' she asked, pointing across the street. 'You can find me there most evenings.'

He bowed and straightened the card with the tips of his fingers, aligning it with the edge of the desk. After she left, Amy wondered if he'd understood. He had said very little to her in English when he'd served her and she had tried to answer him in Japanese. She was suddenly unsure. Toby claimed you needed two thousand words to be able to converse properly in a foreign language, and despite the best efforts of her language teacher, Amy had only managed to retain 379 words of Japanese. And now, for every new word that she added to her total, she would forget one of the old words.

Whether he had understood or not, two days later Koji came to the bar on his way home. He sat by the window looking out into the street but he didn't acknowledge Amy, even though she was certain he had seen her when he walked in. He drank just one beer, and then stood up to leave. She thought to follow him, to watch him stride up the street ahead of her, square-shouldered and slender-hipped. But she didn't. And now another ten days had passed and she still couldn't shake him out of her head: the raven-gloss of his hair, the fullness of his lower lip.

In the bar she always sat behind the armour of her newspaper, yet she scarcely read it. Nori usually talked to her when there was a lull between customers. His English was good, and although Amy thought she'd told him very little, whisky by whisky, late in the evening, Nori had pieced together the story of this lonely British girl. It appeared that her boyfriend, Toby, had dragged her to Nagasaki in the glittering wake of his career, and then left her to her own devices. She made excuses for him: how busy he was at work, and how busy she was with her Japanese classes and her calligraphy lessons. Yet Nori knew that Toby left her alone most evenings whilst he entertained his clients. And he could see that she was sad.

Occasionally one of the customers would say something to Amy, and Nori would translate it into English for her. If it was unrepeatable, then he made something up; he thought of something kinder. Sometimes they simply commented that she looked sad, but Nori never told her that.

'This guy says your hair is like silk,' he said, tonight. She looked up from her book. It was Koji. He sat down on the next stool, twirling a coin between his fingers. When she smiled in acknowledgement, he reached out and touched her hair.

'Shiruku,' he said, nodding.

'Shiruku,' she repeated. Word number 380. He grinned and said something else that she didn't understand.

When Nori returned to translate, she understood that Koji had asked if she wanted another whisky. She thanked him, and Nori lined up two fresh glasses.

Koji finished his drink in two mouthfuls, and each time he lifted his glass she noticed the defined muscle of his forearm. He spoke to her again. It was another question, but all she recognised was the final part - that he was asking her if she'd understood.

'Wakarimasu ka?'

She shook her head and looked questioningly at Nori.

'He wants to know if you'd like to go to another bar.'

Amy finished her whisky, then slid off her stool and held out her hand. Koji blushed and indicated that she should walk ahead. The rain had stopped, and beyond the bright spill of neon signs, Koji guided her down a quiet side street where lantern light from a tea house danced on the cobbles. The red sleeve of a kimono disappeared behind a sliding door, and two voices whispered to each other. There was a promise of something magical in the glistening shine of the wet street.

As they walked, Amy asked Koji questions. He liked cats, and The Beatles. He wrote haiku. And knowing these three things was enough.

When they turned into the next street, he took her hand. 'Ie,' he said, and pointed up at an apartment block. Why was he saying 'no'? Then she remembered. 'Ie' was also the word for home.

'Hai,' she said softly.

They took the lift to his two-room apartment on the fifteenth floor. From the window, Amy could see the lights of the city reflected in the bay like scattered embers. She asked Koji to turn off the lamp, and in the darkness of his room they became each other; skin on skin, as pale as bone, and nothing lost in translation.

THE TEARS OF THE MOUNTAIN CHERRY TREE

As I walk towards the entrance, I notice that the sign has been crudely altered with a black marker. The New Hope Motel has become The No Hope Motel; from a fresh start to total despair with the swipe of a pen.

I look up at the peeling pink stucco, the rusty balcony railings and the rows of faded doors. I know you are behind one of those doors, and right now I'm nervous.

A skinny, tow-haired boy watches me from the corner, throwing a basketball from one hand to the other. As I walk by, he starts to bounce the ball, magnifying the tremor of the subway beneath my feet.

I climb the steps towards a thrum of music; a soft beat marking time inside the first apartment I pass. When I knock on your door, a woman peers out at me from the next one down. A raven plait falls tangled and thick over her right shoulder. She looks like Pocahontas. I nod at her but she turns back inside.

You let me in without a word, into a room that smells of vetiver cologne and stale bacon fat. There's a two-ring stove in the corner with a dirty frying pan sat atop it, and a neat row of empty beer cans lined up at the side of the sink.

'What do you want, Angie?' you say, at last.

'Who's the girl next door?' I ask, ignoring your question. 'Have you replaced me already? It's only four weeks since you left.'

'What's it to you?'

I shrug, and look around. To prove my disinterest, I pick up a postcard that's propped up on the tiny dining table.

'Any chance of a cup of coffee?' I ask.

You nod and reach for the espresso pot, fill it from the tap and spoon in the coffee. I watch your hand shake as you strike a match for the stove. Then you busy yourself with getting the flame right; turning it up to the highest heat possible without the flames licking up the side. But you don't look at me.

You pick up two cups and rinse them out, then you sit down and drum your fingers on the worn formica. I reach out and put my hand over yours to still it. I catch the look in your eyes. The eyes that are still kind. And then I can't speak. I can hear the hiss of the gas, and the faint sound of the music from the room two doors down.

I'm pretty sure you have no idea what I'm going to tell you, but instinctively you know you don't want to hear it.

You trace your finger along a gouge in the table.

'Pete...'

You look up, meeting my gaze again for just a moment, then jump across to the stove as the coffee bubbles through. You pick up the cups and pour the strong, dark liquid.

'Milk?'

I shake my head, and you place one of the cups in front of me and sit back down.

This is so much harder than I dreamt it would be. I planned my speech, I wrote it down and practiced it in my head. And now I don't know what to say.

There's a knock at the door and you scramble to your feet. You only open it a crack, and I hear muted voices. I know that it's your Indian girl. She's been watching and waiting. She knows that I'm still here and she's worried.

I stand up, drink my coffee in a single gulp, and walk over to the door. You jump as I touch your shoulder, and Pocahontas stares at me with those dark, guarded eyes.

'I'll be seeing you around, Pete. Take care of yourself. I'll be in touch.'

I get in my car, but I don't drive away. I still have a decision to make. The same decision I had to make ten years ago.

The breeze blows a cloud of dead petals onto the bonnet of my car; a confetti of dry tears for the end of a marriage. Petals for tears, just like the shower of blossom outside the war museum when we were seventeen. Life was full of possibilities then, unwinding before us like a bright silken thread.

As we ran up the steps to the museum, I reached for your hand and looked up into your eyes. For a few minutes I moved around the vast space, glancing at the uniforms in glass cases, looking up at the fragile planes. The bombs unnerved me. Even in this benign state, their shape instinctively inspired fear.

I stopped at some photographs. The chilling image of a mushroom cloud, bleak depictions of a barren wasteland, glass bottles melted into deformed shapes. Then I saw the plane. Nothing more than a white bomb with wooden wings. Tiny. A single cherry blossom painted on its side. The face of a pilot. A young face. In his funeral portrait, he stares straight ahead. He had kind eyes, like yours.

I squeezed your hand, but I didn't stop reading.

The Yamazakura-tai - the Mountain Cherry Blossom

Corps. Falling blossoms signifying death in battle. Eyes wide open in the face of the enemy. The battle cry: You and I are cherry blossoms in season ... Every flower knows it must die. We will die gloriously, then, for our homeland.

When we stepped back out into the sunlight I walked quietly at your side. I knew that I had to tell you. It was there between us: a tangible thing, unacknowledged, barely formed. It was a new life, and it was life-changing, and I was sure we were too young.

'Pete,' I whispered.

'Yes?'

You looked down at me, and from your eyes I could see that if I told you, you would do the good, right thing. We stopped under a tree, heavy with pale blossom. A soft breeze blew petals onto our hair and shoulders. I thought of the pilot with the kind eyes, about to sacrifice his life, and I knew that I couldn't ask you to do the same.

'Oh, nothing...the museum was sad, wasn't it?' I said, and you brushed away the pink petals along with my tears.

You didn't know that I was about to brush away our baby; a twist of cells, no bigger than a single petal.

I get out of the car and walk slowly back across the forecourt towards your apartment. I've made my decision.

BAREFOOT GIRLS AND CORNER BOYS

It was only last week that I decided to come here, during a rainy Monday afternoon in the bookshop. When Jeanie went to make a cup of tea, I ejected the Vivaldi CD and put on one of yours instead. Your voice swept me across the Atlantic to the Jersey shore, straight into the runaway dreams of all your barefoot girls and corner boys. In an instant I was walking along the boardwalk by the fortune teller's booth, and the waves were crashing onto pale honey sand below.

By the time Jeanie came back down with the tea, I'd made up my mind.

My husband, Max, never liked you. It was pure jealousy; he didn't like anyone who was in my life before I met him. He banned me from playing your music in the house. As with everything else, I fought back at first, and then eventually gave in for an easy life. But Max isn't around any longer, and he has no say about what I do or how I spend my money. So, without hesitation I picked up my coat and headed for the door.

'That's me done for the day,' I said. 'I can't remember if I told you, Jeanie, but I'm taking a vacation and I'm not sure when I'll be back in. I know I can count on you to look after things for me.'

I wish I had a photo to show you the expression on Jeanie's face as I walked out of the door. Maybe it was the word 'vacation' that threw her - the unexpected Americanism. I can picture it now, the way you'll throw your head back in laughter when I describe her.

And here I am, just a week later. I haven't told you I'm coming of course, it will be a surprise. I half-wish there was a friend I could have brought along on this trip, but it's probably best if I see you alone.

The rumour on the internet is that you'll be at Tramps Bar tonight, a mile down the shore. I want to arrive early so I can get near the front and catch your eye straight away.

I eat a chilli dog from the stand opposite the motel, then I buy a bottle of bourbon from the 7-Eleven and place it on the dressing table next to the box containing my new cowboy boots. They have metal wing tips, and the heels are really heavy. I've never owned a pair of cowboy boots before. These are black; lizard skin with contrast stitching. Max would not have approved.

***

The bar is busy and I stand at one end with my beer, tapping out a solid beat to the music with my new heels. The band are good. They're not you, but they're good. Loud. A little like Southside Johnny. I anticipate you stepping out from that small door at the side of the stage. Then the noise of the crowd, cheering loudly when they see it's you. I move closer to the front, take a slug of cold beer. A guy stands next to me in scuffed work boots and a check shirt. He's been here a while, and now I've moved forward he's moved right along with me.

He nods. In that certain way that only American men do,

or maybe only cowboys in films. I know that if he was wearing a hat he would tip it towards me. He strikes up a conversation, asks me why I'm here tonight, where I'm from. We have another beer, and I tell him about you. He laughs.

'You'll sure have a long wait miss, he's playing in Philadelphia tonight.'

I don't mind him laughing. There's something in his laugh that sounds kind rather than mocking, and I feel as though he sees straight through to the heart of me. Either way I like him. And my beer is cold, and the band are good. In fact they're great. They aren't as great as you, but they are great. Nevertheless, I don't give up the hope that you might still walk out on that stage. Because I don't know if Harry - that's the cowboy's name - might be wrong about the Philadelphia thing.

But he isn't wrong. And because you're not here, at the end of the night Harry asks if I want a lift back into town. And so I say yes. He has a red pickup, rusty around the wheel arches, but solid and honest. The radio is turned to a country station. It's loud, but he doesn't offer to turn it down, and he doesn't talk. I look across at him as he's driving. His hair is not unlike yours, and there is something about his broad forearms, his steady gaze. He turns to look at me and I look away, embarrassed, watch the streets go by at the edge of town. A girl in a white dress is standing on a porch and her boyfriend is stepping out of his car. For a moment his eyes meet mine as he crosses the sidewalk, and for one brief second that boy is you.

Then Harry asks me where I want dropping off. Without so much as a pause I look him straight in the eye and I tell him about the bourbon in my room. His eyes crinkle at the corners, just like yours.

CRACKS

The cottage was Alice's idea. It felt less secretive, less like an affair, than signing yet another hotel register as Mr & Mrs Smith.

She had thought of everything they would need. There were tall, slender candles for the dinner table, and her grandmother's silver cutlery and antique glasses. She'd brought two bottles of Greg's favourite wine, some good coffee, and all the ingredients for the dinner she'd planned: a king prawn starter, sea bass for the main course, and a homemade chocolate mousse.

At first, Greg was on edge in the confining rooms of the cottage. The stove had already been lit for them, and he went outside to fetch some more coal from the bunker. When he came back in she told him to sit down, but he wouldn't settle. He drummed his fingers on the chair arm and called through to her in the kitchen, asking what music she would like on.

When the food was ready, Alice lit the candles, and they sat at the tiny table to eat, both of them drinking the crisp white wine a little faster than they should.

Greg kept getting up to tend to the fire, opening and closing the doors, and adjusting the damper. It was burning too brightly and too quickly. Alice worried that it might be the wrong sort of coal for a closed stove. She started to fret that it might crack the glass if it burned too hot. But there seemed nothing for it, whatever he did it continued too fierce and too fast, devouring the coal. Neither of them knew what to do, so they had to let it burn its course.

When they finished the meal, Greg told her that the chocolate mousse was the best he'd ever had. She smiled and said she was glad. He helped her with the dishes and asked her if she would like to go over to the pub.

They went back outside into the cold winter evening and Alice pulled her scarf up over her face. Even in the dark she could make out the white tips of the waves as they lapped the beach, hissing as they withdrew through the sand.

There were hardly any lights in the village. Most of the houses were holiday cottages, abandoned for the winter. Just one or two lamps flickered in the fishermen's cottages down by the slipway, and Alice saw a shadow cross one of the windows. As they walked up the main street towards the pub she could smell the wood smoke drifting from the chimneys.

The pub lights were welcoming; a gentle glow, diffused through the red curtains. Heads turned as the door clattered shut behind them.

There were three fishermen in thick dark jerseys sat at the bar, and an older couple sat in the corner at the side of the fire.

Alice ordered a glass of white wine, but the landlady apologised and said that there was none chilled. Then she asked for a gin and tonic, but changed her mind again when she found out there was no ice and no lemon. Greg shrugged and smiled at the landlady as though it were they that were at fault, and she settled for a pint of local bitter the same as his.

They sat at the other side of the fire and he smiled and took her hand.

'Thank you for this,' he said. 'It was a fantastic idea. Just what we needed, some quiet time together.'

Alice was pleased that he was happy, but was distracted and unsettled by the fishermen at the bar. She was aware of one of them watching her, and when she looked up and met his gaze he didn't look away, but stared, unblinking, his eyes as dark as the night sea. In a way he repelled her; there was something cruel about his mouth and the sharp line of his nose. But she felt compelled to stare back at him.

She moved her chair round so he was no longer in her line of sight, and talked to Greg about what they would do the next day. A trip down the coast to Elmwick Bay, and a meal out in the evening at a restaurant in the next village that she had read about in the guide book. They both got a taste for the beer, and were almost the last to leave the pub, somewhat reluctant to break the spell of their new-found easiness. They linked arms as they walked back down to the cottage, oblivious to the cold.

The fire was still burning when they went in, the coals just glowing now, and the room warm. Greg fetched more wine from the fridge even though they'd both drunk enough already. He put on another of the CDs that he had found in the dresser. Alice didn't know the singer, but the first song was about a woman leaving her man for her first love. Greg caught the look in her eyes before she could compose herself.

'What's the matter, Alice, are you feeling guilty?' he asked.

'Please, Greg, let's not spoil things.' She stroked his hair and leant forward to kiss him, but he pushed her away.

'How can I believe your story? What are the chances of David being at a conference at exactly the same time as you? No wonder you won't ever let me stay at your place - that line about your housemate knowing my wife is obviously just a fob-off.'

'It's about trust, Greg,' she said softly. 'You tell me you don't sleep with your wife any more, and I have to believe you. For my own sanity. Now you have to believe me. I went to Strasbourg on business, not to meet up with an ex-boy-friend.'

She stood up as she spoke and went into the kitchen to make coffee. Greg didn't follow her, and she stood leaning on the kitchen counter, her arms spread wide and her head bowed. She couldn't face this argument again, or any of the others that Greg recalled and reiterated every time he was drunk.

When she went back into the living room he had gone upstairs. She found him asleep on the bottom bunk in the second bedroom. She didn't wake him but went downstairs into the still-warm room, and sat in the soft firelight looking out through the open curtains into the night. The sky was clear and the moon low, and after a while she fetched her boots and coat and went out to the quayside.

There was a light in the fisherman's cottage at the end of the street and she walked towards it. As she neared, the door opened, and she heard the clunk of a lighter and caught the acrid smell of cigarette smoke on the breeze. She could just make out the figure in the dark doorway, see the brightening of his cigarette tip as he inhaled. She didn't turn back but carried on walking until she reached the door. As she drew level he flicked the cigarette away and the glowing tip rolled over the edge of the seawall. Their eyes met, then he turned back inside without a word.

She imagined following him inside. She could see his eyes watching her undress in the lamplight, and feel his calloused hands, rough on her skin, as she fell onto the worn couch beneath him, her arm twisted above her head, and her cheek pressed into the textured moquette.

There was a soft drizzle falling, and as she crossed the cobbles she lifted her face towards the cool rain. She felt detached from Greg, from everything they'd done; suddenly distant from the cold, glittering shame of it. When she went back into the cottage, he had climbed back into their empty bed. She lay still beside him, knowing it was over.

***

The next morning she got up early, woken by the plaintive cries of the gulls. She could see that it was a bright day through the thin curtains, but there was a chill in the air. When she went downstairs there was no sign of Greg. At first she thought he had left, but then she saw him through the back window packing some things into the car.

The living room was cold now; the fire reduced to soft, pale ash.

She pulled on her coat and walked out of the front door before he saw her. She couldn't face him yet. There was a boat high up on the slipway, and one of the other fishermen who had been in the pub was pulling nets and lobster pots up to the top wall. She crossed her arms against the cold and stood watching him for a minute before walking over to the bus stop to read the timetable.

Greg came over and stood beside her, his hands tightly closed as though holding onto something that was anxious to be freed.

'At least have a lift home,' he said, and then he turned back towards the cottage, slowly opening his palms as if silently letting go.

When Alice followed him back inside, she noticed the crack across the glass in the stove door. It ran diagonally from top to bottom, a mere hairline, made visible by the cold light of the winter sun.

SARDINE HERDING

It was almost the end of the English lesson. Mr Richards had asked us all to come up with a sentence that contained a simile. I thought of a story I'd seen on the news: commuters being pushed onto the subway trains in Tokyo by white-gloved station attendants. Herded like cattle, then packed like sardines. Which to use? For some reason I pictured a glittering school of sardines weaving through seaweed, herded by the looming shadow of a hungry shark.

I scribbled down my sentence: *The commuters were herded like sardines into the carriages.*

When I looked up, Mr Richards was at my desk holding out his hand for my paper.

Sandy was in love with Mr Richards, but I couldn't really see the attraction. He was so old, for one thing - at least twenty-six at a guess. He had translucent skin and bony fingers, and wore a battered leather jacket that reeked of stale smoke and fried onions. He smoked roll-ups which he kept in a dented silver tobacco tin. Sometimes our essays would come back with a smear of ash rubbed into the paper.

The bell sounded as I passed him my work, and I raced after Sandy down the corridor.

'Are we going to Derek's tonight?'

Every Wednesday we were allowed to meet up for a couple of hours after we'd done our homework. Our 'O' levels were still a year off, but our parents were really strict about school and stuff. Anyone would've thought it was the 1950s rather than the 1970s, because neither of us was allowed out during the week apart from this. To be honest I'd have rather stayed in on Wednesdays and watched *Survivors*, but beggars can't be choosers. So we both told our mothers that we were going round to each other's houses, when really we always ran down town to Derek's Cafe.

Mr Richards lived opposite the cafe, in the flat above the antique shop. He never closed his curtains, and in winter we could see into his living room. Often he'd sit at his desk in the bay window, marking papers with a cigarette dangling from his lip, occasionally gazing out across the street. Sandy would nudge me and giggle when he looked up, but I don't think she was really sure what she wanted, or what she hoped would happen.

There was the time we never spoke about, when he'd walked into the room completely naked. We stared, wide-eyed, at his smooth, pale chest, his taut buttocks, the line of dark hair that led down from his stomach. We caught each other's eye and blushed, but when we looked up again the room was in darkness. On the way home that night neither of us mentioned what we'd seen, but we'd spotted the glitter and shine in each other's eyes: the new knowing. And as we took the shortcut through the park, the moonlight caught the bare branches of the trees, and I felt something bright and pure race through me - one of those singular moments of teenage clarity when you can imagine the future and know for certain it will be good, and worth the wait.

But for now we were stuck at school, and that future was

still a far-off dream. The present was Derek's on a Wednesday evening; a dimly-lit cafe where conversations were ac-
companied by the constant ding-ding of the pinball machine
and a lingering smell of damp leather and two-stroke oil.
That evening there was only one other customer, a biker
called Joe. I had a massive crush on him, but I hadn't told
Sandy how I felt. He was only a couple of years older than
us - maybe seventeen, or eighteen tops - but I sensed he
thought of me as just a kid.

I watched him lean over the jukebox, his faded red t-shirt
stretched taught across his shoulders. He took his time
choosing, and the first song was half over before he came
back to the table. Derek looked up from his *Racing Post.* 'Not
Neil Young again,' he muttered. Joe smiled, catching my eye.
I blushed, I know I did. He sat back down and took out his
cigarettes and his brass Zippo lighter. I loved that lighter. I
loved the heavy clunking sound it made as it closed, and the
way Joe's hair fell across his eyes when he lit a cigarette.

He often came in the cafe after he'd finished a late shift at
work, and unless his friends were there he would always sit
at the end of our booth. He didn't talk much, but sometimes
his leg would brush against mine. I looked at his strong
hands and felt a stab of something sweet inside, a strange
warmth that melted and slipped away. His eyes were dove
grey, and they crinkled up when he laughed. He wasn't text-
book handsome, but I didn't care.

Before he could open his cigarettes, Sandy slid her tobacco pouch along the table to him, but I reached out for it
before he could take it.

He smiled. 'Maybe Marnie needs the practice,' he said.

I looked up and met his gaze, took a Rizla paper in one
hand and expertly pulled a twist of tobacco from the pouch

with the other. This was something I could do well, something I had practiced. Not too much tobacco, not too little. Not too tight, not too loose. Don't over-dampen the paper. It was my chance to shine, to show him I wasn't some dumb kid.

I held it out to him, blushing, and his fingertips brushed mine as he took it from me.

'Ok, I take it back, Marnie, you're the expert.'

Everyone laughed, and I felt good as I watched him smoke it. But as he stubbed it out in the ashtray he turned to Sandy

'Do you fancy going for a quick spin round the seafront?'

He stood up, as though she'd already agreed, shrugging on his leather jacket. Sandy hesitated for a second and then pushed back her chair.

'Oh yes please! I've never been on a motorbike! Do you mind, Marnie? We won't be long will we, Joe?'

He shook his head and smiled at me as they headed to the door. Sandy zipped up her jacket, fumbling with the spare helmet that Derek had dug up from behind the counter.

I smiled and clenched my fists as the tears welled up, then turned away from the window, waiting until I heard Joe's bike pull away before I snatched my coat from the back of my seat. 'Your tea!' shouted Derek as the door swung shut behind me.

I stood on the pavement a moment, and looked up at Mr Richard's flat. The light was on in his living room but he wasn't sat in the window. I crossed the road and pressed the bell. The intercom crackled.

'Yes?'

'It's Marnie Bridge, Mr Richards. I wondered if I could talk to you a moment?'

There was a pause, then static and throat clearing.

'It's about my homework - the T S Eliot essay,' I added.

The latch buzzer sounded and a light came on inside. I pushed the door into a cold, beige hall. As I started to climb the stairs I saw his pale face looming over the banisters.

The room was warm, heated by a gas fire, and there were piles of books and marking on the floor and table. He cleared a space for me on the settee and stood with his back to the fire.

'How can I help you, Marnie?'

I cleared my throat. I'd no idea what I expected to happen here, I just knew that I had to have something, because Sandy had taken what I really wanted.

'We saw you naked,' I said.

'You did?' He seemed amused.

'It was a couple of months ago. We were in the cafe opposite - that, is Sandy Makefield and I were. We just looked up and saw you.'

He stepped across the room and stood directly in front of me. 'Did you like what you saw?'

He was so close that I could see the green flecks in his eyes, and the rough patch of skin on his left cheek. He took a step back and grinned.

'Sit down, Marnie, relax. Have a cigarette?'

I tried to take one from the tin, my fingers clawing clumsily at the neat rows of roll-ups. I told him they were packed like cattle. He laughed and took one out for me, leaning in with his lighter.

***

The next day I arrived late for English, sliding into the desk next to Sandy's just as Mr Richards called us to attention. I couldn't bear to look at him.

'Where did you go last night?' Sandy whispered. 'We came back after ten minutes but you weren't there? I've something to tell you!'

I didn't answer, pretended to write in my rough book. Sandy scribbled something on a Post-it and pushed it inside the cover of my English book. Mr Richards clapped his hands again and began to discuss the sentences we'd written the day before. His voice jangled in my head and the answers from the other students washed over me. I could still feel his warm breath on my face, and then his lips on mine, soft and greedy. And I could picture Sandy with her arms wrapped round Joe's waist as they sped along the foreshore.

I was suddenly aware that the whole class had fallen silent. When I looked up they were staring at me. A few of the girls started sniggering. I realised Mr Richards must have been calling my name, and I noticed he'd written 'HERDED LIKE SARDINES' on the whiteboard. They obviously hadn't understood I'd written it intentionally, because they were laughing as though they thought I was stupid. Mr Richards caught my eye and winked. I ignored them all and unfolded the Post-it note. I knew it would be about her and Joe, and I also knew I wouldn't be able to tell her what had happened last night.

Joe wants to go out with you but he's too shy to ask! He wanted to check with me first to see if you liked him! I SAID YES! x

'Have you got another example sentence there for us, Marnie?' asked Mr Richards. 'Read it out please.'

I pretended to read from Sandy's note.

'When the girl thought about what happened last night

she felt as sick as a dog.'

My heart was thudding, and I didn't look up. I just flipped the note over and started to write my reply to Sandy.

MICHAEL SECKER'S LAST DAY

Michael Secker stood at the kitchen window and surveyed the clipped and manicured garden that his wife had bullied into submission. His own preference was for an unruly cottage garden filled with overblown peonies; a floozy of a garden that scattered her untidy petals across mossy paths.

Joy swept into the kitchen and broke the spell, observing that if he didn't get a move on he would be late for work.

'I'm sure you wouldn't want that, not on your very last day, Michael.'

It wasn't his official retirement, that had been three years ago; an occasion marked by the presentation of a luxury pergola and matching garden bench.

Michael had wanted a telescope. He yearned to discover comets and meteors, stars and planets, the whirl and glitter of the galaxies opening up possibilities to him from the attic window. If there was a clear sky he would creep up there late at night. He would wait patiently for Joy to put down her gardening magazine and carefully fold her reading spectacles into their case. Then she would turn over onto her side, her hands tucked together as though in prayer, and after a few minutes he would hear the tremulous, gentle snore that signalled eight hours of peace.

He would take his warm jumper from the chair, climb the narrow staircase to the attic and sit in the window on his father's old deckchair listening to the sounds of the house as it settled down for the night. The house stood at the top of a hill, and from the front window the lights of the town winked like strings of fairy lights tangled in a heap across the valley floor. From the attic window at the back of the house the view stretched far across the rolling moors, and at night the skies were black as coal, lit only by fistfuls of milky stars.

Joy had said no to the telescope. She didn't want him up there journeying into space, treading dust and dirt through the house every time he re-entered the atmosphere.

Apparently he was being selfish.

'No, Michael, we need to be thinking of more things we can do together when you retire. I think something for the garden would be nicer.'

As it happened, Joy didn't really take to the pergola as she had hoped. Training plants to wind their way around the latticework so that they were just-so was proving a trial. In fact, the secateurs were now in residence on the kitchen window ledge. Ready to be utilised at a moment's notice with the appearance of each new stray tendril of wisteria.

Michael sat down at the table and opened the newspaper, idly skimming through the blame and shame of the headlines as he waited for his prescribed portion of morning toast.

He heard the scratch and scrape as Joy applied the butter. He was allowed a thin smear, nothing more. 'Cholesterol, Michael, cholesterol.' Any perceived excess was swiftly carried forth to the next slice on the edge of the knife.

Michael looked up as the toast rack was placed before him, the same rack that had graced the table for over forty years. It was replete with triangles as thin as his wife's tightly pressed lips. He folded his paper - reading and eating were not permitted in unison.

'Set you up for the day, that will,' Joy said. 'I'm doing lamb casserole and a Bakewell tart for tea.'

Bakewell had been her maiden name. He had joked with her on their third date that Joy Bakewell was a name that embodied everything a man could wish for: the promise of laughter, happiness and perfect tarts. But Joy had not fulfilled that promise. Maybe it was his own fault for bestowing her with the name Secker. Change just one letter and Joy's name now became her character: Joy Secker the joy-sucker, adept at removing the last shred of pleasure from every experience and occasion.

Things had changed after her miscarriage, and the subsequent discovery that there would be no more babies. Michael had tried not to mind, had tried to be supportive, but Joy built a wall between them. She somehow knew that Michael minded more than she did herself.

He watched now as she perused the garden, her eyes like two black peppercorns beneath furrowed brows. No longer the dark mysterious pools that he remembered from when he first saw her behind the perfume counter at Selfridges.

She opened the kitchen door and peered around the side of the house.

'Mr Jackson's cat is out there again,' she said, and her hand hovered instinctively over the table tennis balls that sat on the window ledge alongside the secateurs.

The balls were there specifically to facilitate the humane despatch of cats, magpies and other undesirables from the garden. Each white ball was marked with a black logo enclosed in a red circle. It gave them the appearance of angry eyes.

Michael had once held them up to his own eyes in an attempt to make Joy laugh. He had been given an unexpected day off, and had grossly underestimated Joy's dislike of the unexpected. She had rejected his suggestion they go out for the day, as appropriate plans hadn't been made. Michael had popped his head around the door while she was hoovering, holding up the balls to his eyes and sporting a manic grin. She lost her temper with him - did he think she had nothing better to do than to lark about? He had better make himself useful and wash the garage paintwork if he was bored.

He remembered that day as he fetched his bicycle from the outhouse. His heart was heavy. Michael wasn't ready to leave Hobson Design, even now. He didn't want to hand his office over to Wayne Noble from quality assurance, or move his bentwood coat stand to credit control as he had promised to do. The truth was that he loved his office and he loved his job. He felt at home there. His office was lived-in, homely and warm. He had his favourite painting on the wall - the wild seascape that Joy had announced did not 'fit in' with their colour scheme - and people knocked on his door before they entered. He felt sure that he commanded a certain respect.

He also enjoyed the relaxed ritual of lunch in the canteen. He was particularly fond of Anita's meat and potato pie on Mondays, and it had to be said that her rice pudding was far superior to Joy's. It was a creamy, luscious concoction, whereas his wife's managed to be both watery and lumpy at the same time.

However, Mr Hobson had been dropping heavy hints.

'You're sixty-eight now, old boy, and you don't know how many good years you have left. Time to think about spending more time with the little lady - time to buy that caravan in Morecambe that she keeps mentioning!'

Michael had never mentioned caravans, or Morecambe for that matter. He was pretty certain that Mr Hobson was confusing him with Maurice Binns in the drawing office. He didn't like to correct him though, so he just smiled and shook his hand.

He considered calling in at the ironmongers on the way home. He needed some bits and pieces for the jobs on his wife's current to-do list. Joy didn't approve of the local ironmongers. She tried to encourage Michael to get the car out and drive to B&Q instead.

'There's a suggestion of something lewd about that Lucy Mount,' she was fond of saying. 'Fancy serving in an ironmongers in high heels and with red polish on your fingernails.'

Michael thought of Lucy Mount's plump, scarlet-stained lips. He loved her smile, and the way it always reached her eyes, the way she looked at him without judgement or disapproval, and the way she listened to him as though he were a man who had something worth saying. He thought of the gentle curves of her body, tantalisingly outlined beneath her tight t-shirt. He sighed.

As he rode his bike out of the driveway he noticed a lone daisy that had dared to rear her pretty head at the edge of the lawn. She was only half awake, and the undersides of her slender white petals were stained pink. Michael was not a gambling man, but if he were, he would have considered it a safe bet to assume that the tiny flower would be despatched to daisy heaven before he returned from work.

However his wife had not yet spotted the horticultural transgression, intent as she was upon the ginger tom cat that had now leapt onto the roof of the garden shed. As quick as lightning she took a ball from the ledge and threw it at the cat through the open kitchen door. The ball missed completely. It glanced off the shed roof and sailed over the high hedge, before hitting Michael squarely between the eyes and sending his bicycle careering into the path of an oncoming car.

As Joy reached for the second ball, she heard the squeal of brakes, followed by a dull thud. Not having her outdoor shoes on she was forced to go into the hallway to fetch them before she went outside to see what had happened.

At the open doorway to the living room her eye was caught by a rumpled antimacassar on Michael's chair back. She went in to straighten it and noticed that the crocheted cloth was looking a little worn. Replacements were hard to come by nowadays, and Joy had been forced to come to terms with the fact that - along with toilet roll covers and pedestal mats - the antimacassar was in serious decline.

She spotted a few other irregularities in the room. There were biscuit crumbs on the carpet by Michael's chair arm, and a rug fringe that had been kicked askew. Engrossed in their correction, she didn't hear the ambulance pull up in the street outside, or see Michael lifted onto a stretcher.

Joy was finally reminded of her original mission by the slam of the ambulance door and the wail of the siren as it pulled away. She went back into the hallway for her outdoor shoes, and as she slipped them on, her husband took his last breath.

Michael Secker didn't fight for his life. He floated upwards, unresisting, through a galaxy of comets and stars until he arrived at the gate of a riotous garden, where a woman bearing a passing resemblance to Lucy Mount was holding out her arms in welcome.

After the policeman and policewoman left, Joy ordered a taxi. She sat in the centre of the back seat, straight-backed, silent and calm, holding her handkerchief in both hands. As they passed through town on the way to the hospital, she suddenly remembered the telescope she had seen the day before in the photography shop window, and asked the driver to stop and wait for her.

The telescope was delivered the day after Michael's funeral, and Joy wasted no time setting it up in the attic. Every evening after Coronation Street she would take her mug of cocoa up the narrow stairs and settle into the deckchair to discover the distant stars. As the galaxies slowly took over her life, the pergola was left to become a tangle of wisteria, the daisies on the lawn were able to go about their daily business uninterrupted, and a thin layer of dust settled on all the horizontal surfaces in the house.

She finally understood what Michael had searched for in the limitless sky. The wild stars, uncontained and disordered, were something that she, Joy, could never tame or muzzle. She had denied Michael this wildness, imprisoning them both in her world of order, beneath a veneer of control that masked her pain. She had been too scared to acknowledge his grief or let go of her own.

And now the stars and constellations had uncovered the depth of her love for him. Sirius and Merga, Polaris and Helvetios, burning as brightly as Joy and Michael once did. Even when their lives were over, stars didn't go quietly or fade to grey, their death rattle was wrapped in a lick of flame. And in each flame she saw Michael.

Sometimes she cried so hard that the only thing visible through the telescope was the bleak void of the years ahead.

ACKNOWLEDGEMENTS

Separated From the Sea would not exist without my brilliant editor and publisher, Amanda Saint. I'm very proud to be the first author signed by Retreat West Books and incredibly grateful to Amanda for all her hard work. She even let me keep a few extra 'ands' against her better judgement!

I'd also like to say a huge thank you to the rest of the RW team, and to the talented Jennie Rawlings at Serifim for her beyond gorgeous cover design.

A massive thank you to my wonderful friends for all their support. However, I daren't name a single one of them, because I'd have to put someone's name first and someone's name last, and they'd all think the list was in order of importance.

Love and gratitude to Mr L, for encouraging me to start writing again, for listening to my stories and ideas, for proofreading, and for always looking after me even when I'm bad.

And a final thank you to my late parents. They were quietly proud of my early writing success, and I know they'd be thrilled to see *Separated From the Sea* published. I'll always be indebted to them for introducing me to the enchantment of stories as soon as I could talk. So this book is for them, and for Fluffy and Duz.

Thanks to the following publishers where some of these stories have appeared previously:

The View Through Rain - by kind permission of InkTears (from *Death of A Superhero* anthology 2017)

Giddy With It - first published by Retreat West Books (*What Was Left* anthology 2017)

Horses - by kind permission of Chapeltown Books (from *Brightly Coloured Horses* 2018)

Already Formed - first published by Valley Press (Walter Swan competition anthology 2018)

All Stations To Edgware - First published in *The Yellow Room* magazine 2012. By kind permission of InkTears (from *Death of A Superhero* anthology 2017)

The Shadow Architect - first published in *Writers' Forum* 2018

To Be The Beach - by kind permission of InkTears (from *Death of A Superhero* anthology 2017)

Just Enough Light - by kind permission of InkTears (from *Death of A Superhero* anthology 2017)

Something Else Entirely - by kind permission of InkTears (from *Death of A Superhero* anthology 2017)

Pink Knickers - first published by Cinnamon Press (from

The Day I Met Vini Reilly anthology 2015)
Tears Of The Mountain Cherry Tree - by kind permission of InkTears (from *Death of A Superhero* anthology 2017)

Cracks - a previous version of this story was first published in *Writers' Forum* 2016

Sardine Herding - first published in *Writers' Forum* 2017

Michael Secker's Last Day - first published by Dragonfly Tea 2016

If you've enjoyed these stories, you can read more from Amanda Huggins, plus many other talented authors, in other Retreat West Books.

WHAT WAS LEFT, VARIOUS

20 winning and shortlisted stories from the 2016 Retreat West Short Story and Flash Fiction Prizes. A past that comes back to haunt a woman when she feels she has no future. A man with no mind of his own living a life of clichés. A teenage girl band that maybe never was. A dying millionaire's bizarre tasks for the family hoping to get his money. A granddaughter losing the grandfather she loves. A list of things about Abraham Lincoln that reveal both sadness and ambition for a modern day schoolgirl.

AS IF I WERE A RIVER, AMANDA SAINT

Kate's life is falling apart. Her husband has vanished without a trace – just like her mother did. Laura's about to do something that will change her family's lives forever – but she can't stop herself. Una's been keeping secrets – but for how much longer?

NOTHING IS AS IT WAS, VARIOUS

A collection of short stories and flash fictions on the theme of climate change. Profits are being donated to the Earth Day Network. A schoolboy inspired by a conservation hero to do his bit. A mother trying to save her family and her farm from drought. A world that doesn't get dark anymore. And a city that lives in a tower slowly being taken over by the sea. These stories and many more make up a poignant collection that is sometimes bleak, sometimes lighthearted, but always hopeful that we can make a change.

https://retreatwestbooks.com